MOCHA AND MANSLAUGHTER

CUP OF JO BOOK 11

KELLY HASHWAY

To Ayla with love

CHAPTER ONE

Cup of Jo, the coffee shop and café I own and run with my now husband, Camden Turner, is hopping Monday morning. Cam and I got married in a very small ceremony here at Cup of Jo on Friday night. My mom officiated, and the only other people in attendance where my father, my sister, Maura—whom everyone calls Mo—and Mo's boyfriend, Wes. Cam and I wanted to keep everything small and intimate. But Bennett Falls is a small town where everyone thinks they're my family, so we recorded the ceremony, and we're playing it all day long today so everyone in town can witness the event.

Mickey Baldwin, one of my best customers, was here first thing after his nightshift at the local high school where he works as a custodian. Seated with him is Mrs. Marlow, who might be my favorite customer. The woman is seventy years old, but she's a spitfire. She even hit a man over the head with a coffee mug to protect me once.

She keeps dabbing her eyes with a napkin as she watches the ceremony for the fourth time on repeat.

Since my two regular employees, Jamar and Robin, covered for Cam and me all weekend so we could take a very short honeymoon to Rehoboth Beach, Delaware, they're both home today, and our newest employee, Tyler Quinn, is here instead. Tyler happens to live with Mrs. Marlow now, which is a situation that works well for the both of them. Tyler needed a place to stay, and Mrs. Marlow needed help around the house since she's a widow. They get along really well, too. They sort of became like an instant family.

Mrs. Marlow stands up from her table and walks over to me at the counter. "Jo, it was such a beautiful ceremony."

"Thank you, Mrs. Marlow. I hope everyone isn't too mad at Cam and me for doing it this way."

She waves a hand in the air. "If anyone complains, you tell them to come talk to me."

"I will." I gently squeeze her arm. "Can I get anything for you?"

"No, but I was wondering if you knew who is leasing the space next door."

She's talking about Bouquets of Love, which, until very recently, was rented by my ex-best friend, Samantha Shaw—or should I say Samantha Perry since she married my ex-boyfriend, Detective Quentin Perry? After Samantha and Quentin betrayed me by seeing each other behind my back while Quentin and I were still together, it's a wonder the three of us can survive in the same town, let alone work next door to each other. Not to mention all the police cases Quentin has roped me into helping him solve. Let's just say it's been more than a little awkward. We all went from really close friends to… I'm not even sure how to put our relationship into words. Everyone in Bennett Falls took my side in the breakup. They also thought I was crazy for tolerating Samantha and Quentin, but truth be told, when their son was born extremely premature, my heart ached for them. I hope the three of them are doing well in their new town.

"Jo?" Mrs. Marlow waves her hand in front of my face. "Joanna Coffee, are you in there?"

"Sorry," I say, shaking my head. "I guess I was lost in thought."

"I hope you aren't sorry to see them go. They've done nothing but cause you trouble."

That might be true, but they were also a big part of my life since childhood. It was a very complicated situation.

An arm slips around my waist, and I turn my head to Cam, who smiles at me. "Are you holding up okay?" he asks me.

"Of course," I say. "I have Mrs. Marlow looking out for me."

"Then I'd say you couldn't be in better hands." Cam smiles at Mrs. Marlow.

Mo walks in with Wes in tow. "Hello to the happy

couple," Mo says as she hugs me. "Are you sure you don't want to take Cam's last name?"

"That was out of the blue," I say as I pull away.

"I was just thinking it might be nice to be the only Coffee girl left in Bennett Falls." Mo bobs one shoulder.

Cam pulls me close to his side. "Jo will always be a Coffee. It runs in her veins."

I highly doubt Mo will change her name if she ever gets married. As much as we were teased as kids for being "Coffee" Coffee, and "Mo'" Coffee—I'll let that sink in for a moment—we've come to love the absurdity of our names.

"I see you're showing the ceremony," Wes says, motioning to the TV screen on the side wall.

"Aw, look how handsome you look in your suit," Mo tells him.

He smiles at her. "I had to look good because I was accompanied by the most beautiful woman I know."

Cam and I exchange a glance. I really hope these two don't rush into marriage. Cam and I literally grew up together, so we didn't wait long after dating to get married. But Mo and Wes haven't known each other for that long at all. Don't get me wrong. I really like Wes, and he's been a great influence on Mo, but it's still too soon for them to get that serious.

Mrs. Marlow waves for me to lean closer, and as soon as I do, she whispers, "I love your sister, but you and Cam make the best-looking couple in town."

I raise one finger to my lips, even though I know Mrs.

Marlow would never say that to Mo. She mimes zipping her lips and throwing away the key.

Mickey walks over to us. "Hey, did you guys hear there's a new police detective in town?"

I shake my head. "I assumed Officer Liberman would become a detective now that Quentin is gone."

"Nope. He's staying where he is. There's a new guy. From what all the women in town are saying, he's easy on the eyes. Latino fellow with a"—Mickey pauses to make air quotes—"'sexy accent.'"

"Who did you hear that from?" Mo asks.

"Who didn't I hear it from? For the women, it was love at first sight, and for the men, it was jealousy at first sight. Cam, Wes, hold on to your ladies."

I raise my left hand and wiggle my ring finger. "I'm happily married. Cam has absolutely nothing to worry about."

He leans down and kisses my cheek. "I need to get back to the kitchen."

I nod.

"We need to get back to the office," Wes says. "We'd better order."

Mo and Wes both work in the office building directly across the street. They're in advertising. Mo is mostly involved in the social media advertising end, but both are wickedly good with computers. Mo can hack into just about anything and dig up information on anyone online.

"I'll get your order for you," I say.

5

"Great. We'll take two mochas, since they're on special today, and two elephant ear pastries."

"Coming right up." I box up the two elephant ears first, and then I brew the espresso and foam the milk for the mocha.

"What exactly is in a mocha?" Wes asks.

"Espresso, cocoa powder, milk, and whipped cream," I tell him as I mix in the cocoa powder and add the milk foam. Then I top it with whipped cream and sprinkle some more cocoa powder on top.

"That looks so pretty," Mo says, taking one of the cups.

"Thanks. It tastes even better," I tell her.

Wes immediately sips his. "Mmm-hmm. Delicious."

"Thanks, Jo." Mo gives a small wave as she and Wes head out.

"So, Jo," Mickey says, "word around town is that the space next to yours is going to remain a flower shop. Is that true?"

"I couldn't tell you, Mickey. I've been away for the past few days."

"That's right." He laughs. "Don't you worry. I'll get to the bottom of this mystery."

"You do that. I'm turning my detective's cap over to you." Now that Quentin isn't part of the Bennett Falls Police Department, I shouldn't need to get involved in any more cases. I can stick to what I do best: serving coffee.

I spend the rest of the morning doing exactly that,

and aside from my honeymoon, it's one of the most relaxing mornings I've had in a long time. I can't help thinking my life is going to be much more enjoyable now that Detective Quentin Perry is gone.

Just before lunchtime, the door opens and a man with a badge displayed prominently on his hip walks in. He matches the description Mickey gave me of the new police detective in town. He marches right up to the counter.

"And you are"—he pauses to consult his notepad—"Joanna Coffee?"

"Yes, that's me."

"And you own this coffee shop?" He looks around, taking in the place.

"That's correct."

"I need to speak with you about your new neighbors."

"Oh, well, I'm afraid I've been out of town. I just got back last night."

"Last night, you say?"

I narrow my eyes, not sure where the detective is going with his line of questioning. "Yes. I was on my honeymoon." I point to the television screen, which is replaying my wedding for about the umpteenth time this morning."

The detective consults his notepad again. "Your husband is Camden Turner, your business partner?"

"Yes." I cross my arms. "Why do I feel like I'm being interrogated?"

"Would you prefer to do this down at the police station?"

"I'm not even sure what *this* is." So far, the new detective isn't making a good first impression on me. I mean, yes, he's attractive in appearance, but his demeanor is lacking warmth. "You haven't even told me who you are."

"Detective Mario Acosta. I'm new to the BFPD."

"Welcome to Bennett Falls, Detective. Can I get you a mocha on the house?"

He looks up, a little stunned by my offer. "Oh, um, I'm working."

"I find caffeine stimulates the brain. It might help." It might also make him ease up a bit and act human. I turn around and start making the mocha.

"I really need to ask you a few more questions."

Cam's head appears in the window to the kitchen. "Everything okay?"

"New police detective." I jerk my head back, and Cam looks in that direction.

"I'm coming out," he says.

A few seconds later, Cam approaches Detective Acosta and introduces himself as my husband. I'm pretty sure I detect a hint of Cam feeling threatened by Detective Acosta's good looks.

I finish making the mocha and place a chocolate straw—a Cup of Jo specialty item—into the cup. "Here you go, Detective. I see you've met my husband." I place my hand on Cam's back.

"Yes, I'm hoping you two can sit down with me for a moment."

I gesture to the corner table, and an odd feeling washes over me. It's the table Quentin and I used to sit at to discuss cases. Don't get me wrong. I don't miss Quentin. It's just odd to have someone who has always been in my life suddenly gone forever.

We sit down, and Detective Acosta hesitantly sips his mocha. His eyes widen. "This is really good."

"Thank you," I say. "Now, what can we do for you?"

"I need to know about the woman renting the space next door."

"Like I said, we've been away on our honeymoon. We haven't met our new neighbor yet."

"Well then, I'm afraid you never will."

"Oh, did she decide not to lease the space?"

"No, she was found dead this morning," Detective Acosta says.

"What? When?"

"Hey, Jo, there are police all over out there," Mickey says, rushing into Cup of Jo for the second time today. I'm surprised he's not home asleep since he works all night. He stops when he sees us with the new police detective.

"Mickey Baldwin, this is Detective Acosta," I tell him.

"Man, you really are good-looking," Mickey says.

"Excuse me?" Detective Acosta looks so confused by the comment I almost laugh, but I remember there's a dead woman next door and stop myself.

"Mickey, you should go," I say, leveling him with a look that I hope conveys he shouldn't get involved.

He walks over to another table.

"Sorry, you're sort of big news in town," I say. "Newcomers always are."

"Right." Detective Acosta clears his throat. "Like I was saying, your neighbor was discovered late this morning. You haven't seen her or anyone next door today?"

I shake my head. "We've been inside the coffee shop all morning. We haven't left, and the space next door was dark when we got here this morning." I want to ask how the woman died, but I don't want to seem too interested in the case.

"I'll need to speak with all your employees. Including those who worked last night."

"We close by six o'clock," I say.

"We don't have a time of death yet, so I need to speak to everyone and anyone who works here."

I can't believe this. With Quentin gone, my days of helping the BFPD with cases were supposed to be over, yet here I am being dragged into yet another possible murder.

CHAPTER TWO

The crowd in Cup of Jo is making their interest in the new police detective very apparent. Everyone has gone completely quiet as they try to eavesdrop on the conversation. Detective Acosta looks around. "Perhaps it's best if we do go to the station after all."

"This is sort of a local hangout in town," I say.

"I can see that."

I wave Tyler over. He looks really timid, which is understandable since his roommate was murdered not long ago, and Tyler was one of the prime suspects. He's not a huge fan of law enforcement in this town.

"Detective Acosta, this is Tyler Quinn. He's new to the Cup of Jo family, and he was not working this weekend. He has been here all morning, though."

"Hi," Tyler says, raising his hand slightly in greeting.

"What time did you arrive here this morning?" Detective Acosta asks.

"Seven o'clock. No, a few minutes before. Like ten minutes early. Right?" He turns to me for confirmation. The poor kid is making himself look really guilty.

"Yes, ten to seven," I say.

"Did you see anyone next door when you arrived?" Detective Acosta asks.

"No. I mean I don't think so. I was focused on Cup of Jo. The specials board was out on the sidewalk, and I was reading it."

"The specials board is on the opposite side of the door from Bouquets of Love, which means Tyler wasn't even looking in the direction of the space next door," I say.

Detective Acosta eyes me, probably wondering why I'm stepping in to speak for Tyler as if he's my son. Being that Tyler is twenty-four and I'm thirty, that's a physical impossibility, but I do feel protective of him.

"Okay, you may go, Mr. Quinn," Detective Acosta says. "Who else was working here last night?"

"Two of my other employees: Jamar Carter and Robin Webber."

"I'll need their contact information."

I take out my phone, but instead of handing over their numbers to Detective Acosta, I call Jamar.

"Hey, Jo," he answers. "How was the honeymoon?" Jamar is not just my employee. He's a good friend and my neighbor in my apartment complex. Our relationship goes beyond employer-employee.

"Jamar, I'm afraid I'm calling because the woman renting the space next to Cup of Jo was found dead this morning. The new police detective wants to talk to you and Robin."

"Oh, wow. Um, okay. Should we come to Cup of Jo now?"

I lower the phone from my mouth. "Do you want them to come here or meet you at the station?" I ask Detective Acosta.

"The station," he says.

"Can you and Robin meet Detective Acosta at the station?"

"Jo, should I be worried?" I can't blame Jamar for asking that question. He's used to having to deal with Quentin, who would have pointed the finger at his own mother if he thought it would close a case faster. I'm really hoping Detective Acosta is nothing like Quentin, though.

"Detective Acosta just wants to know if you or Robin saw the woman or anyone else last night before closing."

"Oh, okay. I'll call Robin, and we'll head to the station right away. Thanks for the heads-up, Jo."

"No problem." I end the call and pocket my phone again. "They'll meet you at the station soon."

Detective Acosta nods. "How well do you know the layout of the space next door?" he asks.

"Decently. Detective, I can't help thinking this wasn't an accidental death or a heart attack."

"I'm not at liberty to discuss the details of the case," he says.

"I understand. It's just that you wouldn't be here if the woman died of natural causes."

"That's an understandable assumption to make." He drinks his mocha and stands up. "I need to get to the station. If you hear anything or remember anything, please call the station and ask for me."

"Of course," I say.

Cam and I exchange a glance as Detective Acosta walks out.

"What do you think?" Cam asks.

"I think that woman was probably murdered."

"I meant about Quentin's replacement."

I cock my head at him. "Camden Turner, are you jealous?"

"No." He scoffs, but I can tell he's putting on a show.

I take his hand in mine. "I think Detective Acosta is better looking than Quentin, but neither has anything on my husband."

Cam smiles. "In case I haven't told you lately, I really love you, Jo Coffee."

"Right back at you, Camden Turner."

"What was that about?" Mickey asks, hurrying over to our table. "The police are all over Sam's old flower shop."

"How did we not hear them?" I ask.

"They aren't using sirens or lights," Mickey says.

"That's strange. Who shows up to a crime scene without at least flashing lights?" Cam asks.

"Maybe the officer who originally responded to the call thought the death was accidental," I say. "And if the woman was dead already, there wouldn't be a need to rush to the scene."

"But who found her and called it in?" Mickey asks.

"I don't know." I don't know anything, and as much as I'd like to say it's for the police to figure out, I can't shake this feeling inside me that's telling me to do my own investigating. "Would you excuse me for a minute?" I stand up, and Cam follows me, leaving Mickey at the table.

"What are you doing, Jo?" Cam asks.

"Calling Mo. We need to find out who died." I dial Mo as I walk into the back office. It's sort of an office-storage area.

"Hey, Jo. Miss me already?"

"Look out your window." Mo's office faces Cup of Jo, so she should have a clear view of Bouquets of Love and the police cars outside it.

"Whoa! What's going on over there?"

"That's what I'm calling you to find out. A woman was found dead inside the store. I need to know who she was."

"How do you expect me to know?"

"She's the new renter."

"Oh, I see. Why don't you ask Mr. DiAngelo?"

Mr. DiAngelo owns this entire strip of stores. He

could tell me who he leased the space to, but he might also tell Detective Acosta that I asked. I'm determined to stay off the police radar now. One thing Quentin let me in on before he moved out of town was that he protected me when it came to the BFPD. I always thought he was throwing me under the bus and was the reason I was interrogated so often, but apparently, it could have been much worse if Quentin wasn't around. Now, I'm completely on my own, and I already know Chief Harvey doesn't hire consultants. He's made that crystal clear on more than one occasion. However, he expects me to hand over any and all information I have to the lead detective on a case. So basically, solve the cases for the BFPD and get no credit or compensation. It's a great deal for him.

"I don't want anyone to know I'm looking into this."

"So you're going to solve yet another case for the BFPD?" She doesn't exactly sound surprised.

"There has to be a reason the new detective is asking questions. If the death wasn't suspicious, he wouldn't be, right?"

"I see your point." The sound of fingers clicking on keys comes through the phone. "Her name is Victoria Masters."

"How did you find that out so quickly?" I ask.

"It's better if you don't ask me things like that. I'm checking her social media profiles now. Hang on."

Since Mo can hack just about anything, I wonder if

she somehow hacked into Mr. DiAngelo's accounts to find out who paid him rent most recently.

"Okay, she turned thirty a little over two months ago. She has really long blonde hair. She's recently divorced. And she just moved to town from New Jersey. Online, everyone calls her Vicky."

"Okay, thanks, Mo."

"Jo, what are you going to do with this information? I mean, do you even know how she died?"

"No, I don't. I just don't want to be blindsided by anything pertaining to this case."

"Is the new detective as gorgeous as everyone is saying?" she asks.

I turn to face Cam, standing beside me. "He's got nothing on Cam and Wes."

"Well, no duh. We snagged to two best guys in town."

"We did. Thanks again, Mo. Let me know if you see anything interesting out your window." I don't want to try to peer out any of my windows because that will look very suspicious.

"Will do." She ends the call.

I want to check on Jamar and Robin, but they probably just got to the station. I'm going to have to be patient, which isn't one of my strengths.

The police finally leave Bouquets of Love around three in the afternoon. After the last patrol car pulls away, I go into the kitchen to talk to Cam. "I want to go next door and check out the crime scene."

"Why? Jo, you can't go anywhere near it. If someone catches you…" He sighs. "I hate to say this, but you don't have Quentin to back you up anymore. This new detective doesn't know you at all. He won't hesitate to accuse you of something."

"Quentin never hesitated either."

"He did what he had to so he didn't raise suspicion with the chief, but he never let any charges stick."

That's true. "I need to know where and how this woman died."

"Why? Let the police do their jobs. They get paid for this. You don't." He finishes cleaning the island countertop and walks over to me. "Besides, it's broad daylight. Someone can easily see you go over there."

He's right. If I want to go over there, I'll need to wait until it gets dark. "Okay, then I'm calling Jamar to see what he knows."

"That's a much better plan. Why don't you invite him over for dinner tonight? Robin, too?"

"Good thinking." I text Jamar to invite him over.

He doesn't respond right away, which makes me worry more. What if Detective Acosta still has him and Robin at the station? Did one of them see something? I didn't get a chance to ask Jamar when I called him because Detective Acosta was sitting at the table with me.

I never thought I'd miss Quentin, but if he were still here, I could get the information I need. Now, I feel completely in the dark. And if a murder really did happen right next door, I want to know as much about it as possible. Should I be scared to be at Cup of Jo?

The last few hours of work crawl by. I'm going through the motions. Luckily, Tyler is great. He's taking care of most of the customers for me while I try to keep my mind occupied by cleaning the display cases and tables. I really lucked out finding Tyler. I have the best employees I could ever ask for. And I'm really glad that hiring Tyler means I can finally give Jamar and Robin days off. I was overworking them, and it made me worry one of them—if not both—would wind up quitting on me.

Finally, six o'clock rolls around, and Cam and I close up for the day.

"See you tomorrow," Tyler says before he gets in his car, which is parked beside Cam's SUV.

"Bye, Tyler," I call to him.

I mentally go through the contents of the refrigerator as we drive home, but considering our apartment complex is only one mile from Cup of Jo, I don't get much time to think about it. Midnight, the resident black cat who wanders between all the apartments in the building, is waiting for us on my welcome mat.

She meows, letting me know she expects dinner as well. I open the door and immediately get some tuna and fresh water for her. Then I search the refrigerator. I have everything to throw together some tacos, so I get started on that right away. I still haven't heard from Jamar, and that worries me more than I'd like to admit. His apartment door is closed, which is a tell-tale sign he's not home. We all keep our doors open when we're home so Midnight can come and go as she pleases.

As I cook, I listen for footsteps in the hallway. I'm putting the food on the table when Jamar walks into the apartment.

"Hey," he says, looking haggard.

"Are you okay?" I put down the bowl of shredded lettuce and turn to him.

"Long day. Robin went home to shower. She'll be here in about half an hour."

"Were you at the station that whole time?" I ask.

He nods. "The new detective insisted on talking to everyone individually."

"Everyone?" I ask. "Like who?"

"Me, Robin, a delivery guy who dropped off a package to the new renter, everyone at the company who brought in the shipment of flowers yesterday, you name it."

Jamar looks like he's about to collapse, so I pull out a chair for him. "Sit."

He does and immediately reaches for some lemonade. "Thanks."

"So, the new renter was keeping it a flower shop?" Cam asks as we take our seats.

"Yeah, from what I heard, they were planning to keep the name, too." Jamar begins to prep his tacos on his plate.

"According to Mo, Vicky Masters moved to Bennett Falls after getting divorced," I say as I add cheese to the taco I'm assembling.

"So maybe she was running from a bad marriage, and her ex-husband followed her here," Jamar says, his mouth full of food.

"I'd say looking into the ex is always a good place to start."

CHAPTER THREE

I tried to give Robin and Jamar the day off since they had such a rough time at the police station yesterday, but both insisted it was best for them to stay busy and continue with work as usual. Mickey had them cornered all morning, questioning them about the new detective in town and the murder. If that's what it was. According to Mickey, the police are disputing that theory.

"If it were Quentin investigating this case, he would have shooed this under the rug and gone with the accidental death angle," I tell Cam as we talk through the window into the kitchen.

"Mickey said it's actually Detective Acosta who is pursuing this as a possible homicide."

"Yeah. He thinks it looks suspicious. The others at the station think Vicky Masters didn't know anyone here, so she wouldn't have any enemies to want her dead."

"That does make sense. I'm a little surprised Chief

Harvey is allowing Detective Acosta to pursue this so hard." The timer goes off behind Cam, and he hurries to the oven to remove a tray of scones.

"Chief Harvey might be testing Acosta," I say once Cam has returned. "You know, trying to see what kind of detective he is and what level of grief Acosta will cause him."

"That's true. I could see Chief Harvey doing that. Especially after dealing with Quentin for so long."

Quentin Perry was a good detective, but between covering for me when my investigative tendencies got me into trouble and dealing with the early birth of his son, he was more than a little off his game for the past few months.

"You're wondering how they're doing, aren't you?" Cam asks, one side of his mouth curling up in a sympathetic smile.

"It's more curiosity than anything else."

Cam walks out of the kitchen and wraps his arms around me. "No, it's you being you. You can't stop caring about people, even when they don't deserve your concern."

"I'm an idiot."

"No, you're not. Don't ever say that. You're the best person I know." He kisses the tip of my nose.

"Hey, Jo," Robin says. "Heads-up. Mickey saw the new detective coming this way."

Cam releases me but stays by my side. I'm not sure it's a good idea to look like we knew Detective Acosta was coming. We don't need to give him any reason to suspect us of something.

"Thank you, Robin. Everyone back to work." I turn to Cam. "You too. Back in the kitchen. We have nothing to hide."

He hesitates, but then he walks into the kitchen. Through the window, I see he's staying close to the door in case he needs to come back out here in a hurry. I'd expect no less from him.

"Detective Acosta might be really attractive, but he's out for blood," Robin says. "Be careful, Jo. You and Quentin had a history. This guy isn't going to take you putting him in his place the way Quentin did."

Quentin didn't have a choice but to take grief from me. He cheated on me, ruined our relationship and our friendship, and falsely accused me of murder more than once. He should have bought me a new car or something before he left town.

"I can handle it. Don't worry about me, Robin. I'll be fine."

She smirks. "Oh, I know you'll be fine, but I don't want to have to come bail you out of jail for punching the new detective in the face."

"Believe me. If I never punched Quentin in the face, Detective Acosta has nothing to worry about." Going to jail for assaulting an officer of the law might have been worth punching Quentin, though.

Robin goes into the kitchen, most likely to see if Cam has any pastries for the display case. She's taken it upon herself to help him refill the display cases throughout the day. The door to Cup of Jo opens, and Detective Acosta steps inside. He looks around, as if taking in the clientele. It doesn't really change much from one day to the next. People in Bennett Falls are creatures of habit. If a resident has lived here long enough, I could tell you exactly where they'll be on any given day at any given time.

Detective Acosta walks up to me. "Ms. Coffee—or should I call you Mrs. Turner?"

"I haven't changed my name, but it doesn't bother me either way."

He dips his head in response. "I'd like to speak with you some more, if you don't mind."

"Can I get you something to drink?" I ask.

"Um..." He seems taken aback by the offer. "Whatever that was you gave me yesterday would be great. Thank you."

"One mocha, coming right up."

"Thank you." He walks over to the table we sat at yesterday.

"What's he doing back here?" Cam asks through the window.

"I'm not sure yet. He only said he wants to talk to me more."

"About what? You never even met this woman." Cam's annoyance comes through loud and clear.

"I don't know. I'll give you a signal if it isn't going well." I'm sure he'll be watching through the window the whole time.

"Touch your nose if you need me to come out there," he says.

I bob my head as I finish making the mocha for Detective Acosta. I bring it to the table for him and sit down.

"None for you?" he asks me as I place the mocha in front of him.

"If I told you how much coffee I consume throughout the day working here, you'd probably faint."

He smirks. "I guess I can believe that." The way he says it makes me wonder if he's trying to judge whether or not I'm trustworthy.

"What brings you here again today?" I ask, trying to keep my tone casual.

"I have a few more questions for you."

"Detective, I'm going to level with you. Word around town is that the police aren't sure whether or not the woman next door died of suspicious causes or if it was an accidental death."

"Word around town?" he asks.

I lean my elbows on the table in front of me. "You're new to Bennett Falls, so I'll let you in on a secret. It's a small town. Word travels fast, and it usually happens right here. Cup of Jo is a local hangout."

He looks around again. "I can see that. I don't suppose you'd point me in the direction of the town's biggest gossips, would you?"

"Are you scouting out potential C.I.s?"

He cocks his head at me. "What do you know about confidential informants?"

I let out a loud huff. I have no doubt Detective Acosta will look into me, if he hasn't already. This very well might be a test to see if I'll be honest with him. "I used to date the detective you replaced. It was years ago, but I sort of got the detective bug from him."

"Did he talk to you about his cases?" He sips his mocha, eyeing me over the rim of the glass.

I need to tread carefully here. While Chief Harvey can't fire Quentin anymore, if Detective Acosta tells the chief that Quentin used to feed me information about his cases, he could easily make a call to Quentin's new superior and make his life difficult. I admit there was a time when that would be really tempting, but with Quentin Junior in the mix now, I'm not going to jeopardize Quentin's job. That baby is going to need a lot of care for a while.

"Detective Acosta, I don't like what you're implying."

"I'm not implying anything. I'm merely asking questions."

"Okay, then I'll tell you that my relationship with Detective Perry was strained at best. If you do some digging, you'll find he interrogated me several times. Our previous relationship didn't end well either."

"Yet you catered his wedding," he says with a smug smile. I'm sure he thinks he's caught me in a lie.

"I was tricked into that. But I fail to see how my personal life is important to your case, Detective. Or is it possible you're looking to become the new town gossip?" Okay, I know I'm teetering on getting on the detective's bad side with that comment, but come on. It's become glaringly obvious he's trying to set me up here, catch me in a lie. I'm not letting that happen.

"Ms. Coffee, I don't play games. You and I do not have a relationship, nor did we ever, so I strongly caution you to remember I'm not Detective Perry."

"I'm sure we're both thankful for that," I say, trying to lighten the mood.

He clears his throat, something Quentin did all the time when he was uncomfortable, which was often when he was around me. "Did you ever assist Detective Perry with a case?"

"If you'd like to know about my involvement with the BFPD, I suggest you speak with Chief Harvey." *I can play hardball, too, Buddy!*

"Very well, I will."

I have to resist the urge to roll my eyes at his weak attempt at intimidation. "Good. Are we finished here then?"

"Not even close. Tell me what you know about Victoria Masters."

"Nothing." I shrug.

"You're sticking with the assertion that you didn't know the victim at all?" he asks.

"Yes, because that's the truth. I never met her. I couldn't even pick her out of a police lineup." That's true, too. Cam and I spent most of the night talking to

Jamar and Robin, but they were too wiped out from everything Detective Acosta put them through during the day that I didn't want to do any research of my own with them present. And since they stayed pretty late, it left me with no time for anything before I crawled into bed for the night. Other than what Mo told me yesterday, I don't know anything about Vicky Masters.

"Then how do you explain this?" Detective Acosta pulls a piece of paper, roughly the size of a sticky note, from his pocket and slides it to me. On it is my name.

"What is that?"

"Your name," he says as if I'm a complete idiot.

"I can see that, Detective. What I can't see is why a piece of paper with my name on it is important."

"We found this on the counter in Bouquets of Love."

"Then it was probably leftover from the previous owner, Samantha Perry. I knew her."

"Knew her well enough to know her handwriting?" he asks.

Yes, I did. Sam and I were best friends for many years. We wrote notes to each other in school since the high school has always had a "no cell phone" policy. I bob my head.

"Are you positive this is Samantha Perry's handwriting?" he asks.

I look more closely at the note. The handwriting is similar but different. If Samantha had been scribbling it in a hurry, then I'd say she wrote it. But if not... "I can't say for sure, but it does look like her handwriting."

"Why would she write down your name if you're friends? It seems to me that you write down something because you need help remembering it."

Samantha wasn't very good at remembering things. At all. But I'm not going to get into that with the detective. "I placed orders for flowers sometimes. I bought some arrangements for Cup of Jo." I never actually placed that order. It was supposed to be a charade to keep Quentin from finding out that Sam and I were discussing a case behind his back. But Samantha didn't exactly catch on to that and put the order through anyway.

"It's not an invoice."

"Samantha didn't always do things the way other people did. Ask around town. She was a very unique individual."

"Okay, then how about this?" He pulls out another piece of paper. This time it only has one word written on it. *Mocha.* "I found this beside the note with your name on it." He raises his drink in his hand. "What did you say this was called?"

He set me up.

CHAPTER FOUR

I can't believe this. I have no idea why someone would write the word mocha on a sticky note or why this woman might have jotted my name on one either. I reach up and scratch my nose. It's possible Cam breaks a world sprinting record with how quickly he is out of the kitchen and at my side.

"Detective Acosta, I didn't realize you were here," he says.

Detective Acosta's gaze volleys between Cam and me. "Yes, I'm sure you would have been out here much sooner if you had."

"Detective, I'm afraid I don't see where you're going with your questioning. This piece of paper means nothing to me."

"It doesn't?" He furrows his brow and sucks his lips into his mouth. "Interesting, because it happens to be the drink you had on special the day Victoria Masters was found dead."

"Coincidence," Cam says.

"I don't believe in coincidences, Mr. Turner," Detective Acosta says.

"Really? I would expect a detective to consider every possibility." The way Cam says it, it's clear he's questioning Detective Acosta's skills.

"Detective, I don't choose the specials until that morning. There's no way Ms. Masters could have known what the special would be before she died since I myself didn't know."

"Or maybe you saw this note, and it's what gave you the idea."

Even I have to admit that's a smart theory, one Quentin wouldn't have come up with. "I never saw that piece of paper."

"Maybe you didn't realize you saw, and your subconscious mind told you to make mochas the special yesterday."

"There's a big flaw in your theory, Detective." I lean forward and stare directly into his eyes. "I haven't been inside Bouquets of Love in weeks."

"I can vouch for that," Cam says.

Detective Acosta places the two pieces of paper side by side. "Would you say the handwriting matches?"

They definitely do, and it's now clear to me that Samantha didn't write these. The M in mocha doesn't match Samantha's style of writing. I'm not going to tell

Detective Acosta that, though. "I'm not a handwriting analyst. I believe that BFPD has people who are. I suggest you talk to them."

He smiles as he picks up the pieces of paper. "Oh, believe me; I will."

Something strikes me as odd. "Detective, if you believe those pieces of paper are evidence of something, why are you handling them so carelessly? Shouldn't they be in evidence bags?"

He stands up, pocketing the papers in the process. "Let me worry about my evidence, Ms. Coffee." He picks up what's left of his drink and finishes it. "Mmm, delicious mocha." I know he's repeating the name of the drink for my benefit. "Have a good day. I'm sure I'll be in touch."

Once he's gone, Cam wraps an arm around my waist. "I never thought I'd say this, but I actually miss Quentin."

"Right now, so do I."

Mo and Wes show up in the early afternoon for a coffee break. I fill them in on my conversation with my new least favorite person in town.

"What a jerk!" Mo shakes her head. "I hate it when guys are gorgeous and think that means they can treat people like trash."

Wes turns in his seat to give Mo major side eye. "You think Detective Acosta is gorgeous?"

"Oh, come on. You have eyes. You've seen him. He's like the definition of tall, dark, and handsome with the added bonus of a sexy accent."

"You're digging yourself a pretty deep hole there, Mo," I say as I watch Wes's face. The guy is clearly jealous.

"Okay, but it doesn't matter how attractive someone is if they're a complete jerk. It instantly makes them ugly."

"So now he's ugly?" Wes asks.

"Totally." Mo looks at me. "You get what I'm saying, right?"

I do. "Beauty isn't skin deep."

"Exactly. That man is uglier on the inside than Quentin Perry, and coming from me, that's a big insult." Mo never liked Quentin, not even when he and I were dating. She's always been team Cam. She even had a crush on Cam when we were kids.

"All right, I'll let it slide," Wes says.

"Anyone have any idea why Victoria Masters would have written my name on a piece of paper?" I ask.

"Wait." Mo holds up a hand. "Where was Detective Acosta sitting?"

"Why?" I ask.

She looks under the table. "He could have bugged this place."

"I don't think he'd do that."

She stands up and checks under her chair. "You don't know anything about him, Jo. A problem I plan to rectify, by the way. You're cooking dinner tonight, right?"

"Pulled pork. It's in the slow cooker as we speak."

Wes rubs his stomach. "Yum!"

"Great. We'll be there." She swats my leg aside to look under my chair.

"Stop searching for bugs. Detective Acosta was sitting exactly where you are, anyway."

"If he was smart, he would have put the bug on Jo," Wes says. "Then it would go everywhere she did."

"No one bugged me, and I'll prove it." I dip my head down. "Detective Acosta is an incompetent cop who will never figure out I murdered Victoria Masters."

"Jo!" Mo shrieks. "Don't even kid around about things like that."

"I'm just proving a point. I'm not bugged. Detective Acosta would be barreling down Main Street right now to arrest me if I were."

"For all we know, he's on his way," she says.

"Please focus. We need to find out why Victoria Masters knew my name when I didn't know hers."

"And why she wrote the word mocha on that other piece of paper," Wes says.

"When are you talking to her ex-husband?" Mo asks.

"When you get me his phone number and address," I say.

"Oh, sorry. It's been a busy morning. I meant to text that to you." She whips out her phone, and a moment later, mine vibrates in my pocket with a notification.

"Thanks. Cam and I will go check him out."

"He lives right over the border in New Jersey."

"Good, then it won't take long to get there."

With Robin and Jamar taking care of things at Cup of Jo, Cam and I head to Columbia, New Jersey. Being that it's a Tuesday afternoon, I'm not counting on Thomas Masters being home. But maybe one of his neighbors will be. I need to get a sense of what this guy is like and if he'd be angry enough with his ex-wife to want to kill her. If Thomas and Victoria lived in this house together and went through a messy divorce, there's a very good chance the neighbors overheard some arguments.

Thomas Masters's house is an old Victorian. It was probably gorgeous back in the day, but it's clearly lacking in upkeep. Cam pulls into the driveway and parks. There's no car visible, but we ring the doorbell anyway. Like we expected, nobody answers. We start walking back to Cam's SUV when two female power walkers head our way.

"Excuse me," I say, waving to them.

The two women, I'd guess in their mid-forties, exchange a glance before walking over to us. "Yes?" the taller of the two asks.

"Hi, we were wondering if you know the man who lives in this house, Thomas Masters?"

The shorter woman rolls her eyes. "He's a piece of work, that man."

"Can you tell us about him?" Cam asks.

"He's one of those men who think women are inferior in every way," she continues as she crosses her arms.

"Poor Victoria," the taller woman adds. "I never understood how she put up with him. He was always yelling about something. The way she cut the grass, the way she packed his lunches for work, the way she washed the windows…" She shakes her head. "Don't even get me started on his comments about her clothing. What right did he have to tell her how to dress?"

The shorter woman wags a finger in the air. "I'm telling you it's because he was so much older than Vicky. Twenty years!" she says, directing the statement at Cam and me. "He's fifty. Vicky's only thirty. She could do so much better than him. I'm just glad she finally came to her senses and left him. I hope wherever she is now, she's much happier." She scoffs. "Though I really don't see how she can't be. Not having Thomas in her life is a huge improvement on its own."

"I hate to tell you this," I say, "but Vicky is dead."

"What?" both women shriek.

Cam bobs his head. "She was renting the flower shop next to our coffee shop. The police found her Monday morning."

"How did she die?" the taller woman asks, raising her hand to her mouth in horror.

"She fell down the stairs and broke her neck."

The women exchange glances. "He was out of town, wasn't he?"

"I don't recall. I don't think we saw his car Sunday evening."

"He must have followed her there."

The shorter woman has tears in her eyes. "They probably fought, and he pushed her. How else would she break her neck?"

Detective Acosta needs to know about this, but I can't be the one to tell him. "Ladies, I know the name of the detective with the Bennett Falls Police Department who is in charge of Victoria's case. Would you mind calling him and telling him what you know about Thomas? I think Detective Acosta should speak to him."

"Bennett Falls?" the taller woman asks. "That's not that far from here."

"About forty minutes," I say.

"He would have had time to kill her and come home," the shorter woman says.

"It's clear you think Victoria had a reason to fear her ex-husband," Cam says. "Did you ever witness anything that made you think he'd physically abused her?"

The shorter woman starts to cry, but the taller one gets angry. "She had bruises. Mostly on her arms. She wore long sleeves in every kind of weather to cover them up. We only saw them because she used to walk with us sometimes. She stumbled once on some uneven pavement. Cheryl grabbed her arm to keep her from falling, and Vicky winced."

The shorter woman, Cheryl, nods. "She tried to pull

away, but I pushed up her sleeve and saw the bruises myself."

"You need to tell all of this to the detective in charge. If Thomas hurt Vicky before, there's a chance he had something to do with her death."

"You said it was the Bennett Falls Police Department," the taller woman says, taking her phone from the side pocket of her running pants.

"Yes. The detective's name is Acosta. But please, don't mention that Cam and I talked to you."

The taller woman cocks her head. "Why not?"

"He found a piece of paper in Vicky's new flower shop with my name on it. I can't explain it, but he thinks it's making me look guilty of something."

"But you didn't even know Vicky. What reason would you have for wanting to hurt her?" she asks me.

"Grace, we need to help her. We both know Thomas is the likely suspect," Cheryl says.

Grace bobs her head. "Don't you two worry. We'll say we heard about this on the news. It's been on the news, right?"

"Yes," Cam says. "The media hasn't released many details at all, but Vicky's name was in the news."

"Okay, then," Grace says. "We're going to call this detective right now. I suggest you two get far from Columbia in case he wants to come here to talk to us."

"Thank you," I say.

"No need to thank us. We're doing this for Vicky. She deserved so much better, and if that lowlife did kill her, I want to make sure he spends the rest of his sorry existence behind bars."

Cam and I say goodbye to the two women and head home. Jamar and Robin are closing up Cup of Jo, so I go home to check on the pork in the crockpot.

Around six fifteen, Mo, Wes, Jamar, and Robin all arrive. I'm not surprised Jamar came, but Robin is a bit of a shock to me. While she's become part of our inner circle, she does date our friend Lance, who owns an upscale restaurant in Highland Hills. I'm used to her being with him in the evenings.

"I hope it's okay that I came," Robin says, handing me a bottle of wine.

"Of course. You're always welcome," I say.

"Lance says hi. The restaurant is fully booked with reservations this evening." That explains why she's here.

"Tell him hi back. He's been so busy lately I feel like we haven't seen him in forever. That's great, though. I'm glad the restaurant is doing so well." Lance has had a really rough life. His father walked out on him and his mom when Lance was a child, and his mother is currently serving time in prison. It's a wonder Lance turned out to be such a sweet guy, not to mention a very talented chef.

"Yeah, he's doing really well." She sounds almost sad about it.

"You miss him," Mo says.

Robin smiles, but it's a sad smile. "I do. I don't see him much either."

I hope things get better for them soon. I really like having both of them in my life. I wouldn't want things to end badly between them and our circle of friends to have to change because of it. That almost happened in the brief time Robin and Jamar tried to date. Thankfully, they've remained friends.

We eat dinner, and Cam and I fill everyone in on our conversation with Cheryl and Grace this afternoon.

"Sounds like the ex-husband is the guilty party," Mo says. "It's almost cliché."

"We don't know for sure that it was him," Jamar says, "but even if it's not, I hope Detective Acosta is hard on him. No man should ever get away with hitting a woman."

"I knew I liked you," Mo tells Jamar.

"I think we should look into Thomas Masters," I say.

"In other words, dinner is over. Time to get to work," she says, standing up and bringing her plate to the sink.

"I'll load the dishwasher," Jamar says. He and I have talked about him coming over and acting like an employee instead of my friend, but he's assured me he does this at all his friends' places. I've stopped arguing with him.

"Thanks, Jamar."

"I'll help you," Robin says, heading to the kitchen with him.

The rest of us go into the living room to get comfortable. We each get on our phones and divvy up Thomas Masters's social media profiles. All except Mo, who is looking into the details of the divorce. Don't ask how. Her methods aren't always totally legal, so I've found it's best not to ask questions and to pretend it isn't happening.

"It looks like Victoria took out a restraining order against her ex-husband. Or tried to. She dropped it." Mo shakes her head. "Why would she drop it if he assaulted her?"

"I don't know. Maybe she was scared of him, and he threatened her." It's the only thing I can think of. "She might have thought moving out of town would be good enough because she was putting distance between them."

"Forty minutes isn't much distance," Wes says.

No, it's not, and that might have gotten her killed in the end.

"Thomas Masters used to be a mixed martial arts fighter," Wes says. "He gave it up when he was thirty-seven, but I'd say he most likely was still a strong guy."

"It doesn't take a lot of force to push someone down the stairs," I say. "I'm not sure that matters much."

"You're probably right. He works in sales now for some computer software company."

My cell phone rings, interrupting the conversation. I'm startled by it since I'm using my phone to research, and I forget to look at the number before answering. "Hello?"

"Ms. Coffee?"

I recognize Detective Acosta's voice. "Yes?"

"I need you to come to the station first thing in the morning."

"What for?"

"I got an interesting phone call today from two women who live in Columbia, New Jersey."

"Did you?"

"Yes, it seems they lived by Victoria Masters and her ex-husband."

"Oh, well that's good news. I'm sure they had some useful information for you."

"Yes, and oddly enough when I asked them how they knew to contact me, they said they heard about Victoria in the news. The funny thing is my name wasn't mentioned in relation to the case."

"Oh?" Why wouldn't he be mentioned if he's the lead detective on the case? "Why is that?"

"I find it's easier to investigate when my name isn't plastered across the news. So the question remains, how did these women find out about me, especially since I just moved to Bennett Falls, and this is my first case with the BFPD?"

"That is a mystery, but you're the detective. I'm sure you'll puzzle it out."

"I believe I already have. I'll see you first thing tomorrow morning." He pauses. "Sleep well, Ms. Coffee. I have a feeling you're in for a long day tomorrow."

CHAPTER FIVE

Even though Detective Acosta didn't ask Cam to come to the station Wednesday morning as well, Cam accompanies me. I'm pretty sure Detective Acosta caught on to the fact that Cam and I are a package deal long before Quentin ever did. It still amazes me that Quentin thought I'd keep information about cases from Cam. I don't keep anything from Cam. He was my best friend long before he became my boyfriend or my husband.

I haven't been to the Bennett Falls Police Department since Quentin left, and it feels a little strange walking in here knowing he won't be there. Chief Harvey is in his office, but the door is open, so I catch a glimpse of him as we pass. He's at his desk looking over some paperwork. He looks up briefly at me but doesn't nod or acknowledge me in any way.

I automatically head in the direction of Quentin's

desk, but I see it's empty. I assumed Detective Acosta would take over that space, but it seems I was wrong.

"Ms. Coffee, over here."

I turn to see Detective Acosta standing outside an interrogation room. He's seriously going to question me in there instead of at a desk. The nerve of this man. It's not like I'm a suspect. He's just annoyed I'm looking into this case.

"Where's your desk, Detective?" Cam asks as if reading my mind. "I think that would be more than sufficient for us to talk."

Detective Acosta's gaze goes to Chief Harvey's office. He clearly wants privacy. But why? He's not trying to protect me. Is he afraid I'll make him look bad in front of his new boss?

"It's fine," I tell Cam, trying to show no fear, although I'm really not sure yet if I should be afraid of Detective Acosta. I don't know enough about him.

Detective Acosta steps aside and gestures for us to go into the interrogation room. "From what I've heard, you've been here before."

He's trying to trap me. I can't admit to helping Quentin solve cases. Chief Harvey did his best to cover up that fact since he doesn't want to use consultants. I can't come out and tell Detective Acosta I interrogated witnesses with Quentin. Nor do I want to let him think I've been interrogated in here as a suspect. I quickly come up with a better idea.

"There might have been instances where people requested my presence in this room while they were interrogated." That happened rather recently when my newest employee, Tyler, was questioned in connection to his roommate's murder.

"Yes, well, a certain former police detective broke a lot of rules around here, but that's not going to happen anymore. I plan to follow proper police procedures at all times." He gestures to the chairs since Cam and I are both still standing.

I sit, and Cam follows my lead. "Why are we here, Detective? I can't help thinking your efforts would be better spent interrogating actual suspects in the case."

Detective Acosta sits down and leans across the table. "Let me be very clear. I plan to stay in Bennett Falls for a very long time."

"It's a great town," I say, determined to not let him see me squirm.

He pauses but only for a second. "I'd appreciate it if you didn't interrupt me."

I motion with my hand for him to continue.

"Tell me why you were in New Jersey yesterday."

"What makes you think I was?" I ask. He could have checked up on us since we did pay tolls both entering and exiting New Jersey. I want to find out if he went through the trouble to do so.

"Are you denying the little trip you made to Columbia?" he asks.

"All I asked was why you think I'd go there." I'm careful not to say we, but I'm not sure there's any reason to be since it's pretty clear Cam and I do almost everything together.

"I think you spoke to two women. Do the names Cheryl Ziegler and Grace Marsh ring any bells."

"Are they actors?" I ask, turning my head slightly to Cam. "They sound like names of actors, don't they?"

"They definitely do." Cam bobs his head.

"Do you want me to run your plate and look into your whereabouts yesterday?" Detective Acosta asks.

"What I want is to know what this is really about," I say. "Why are we here? You have a case to solve, yet you're keeping two coffee shop owners from work instead of finding out how Vicky Masters died."

"Vicky?" Detective Acosta says. "I thought you didn't know the victim."

"I didn't."

"Yet you called her Vicky instead of Victoria, as if you were friends or at the very least acquaintances."

"We knew a girl in high school named Victoria. Everyone called her Vicky," Cam says, and it's not a lie.

"Ms. Coffee, I need to know what you're up to." Detective Acosta laces his hands on top of the table. "I know you were in New Jersey. I know you're asking a lot of questions about Victoria Masters. What I don't know is why?"

"Detective, I think you've jumped to a lot of conclusions, both about this case and about me." When he opens his mouth to protest, I keep pushing on, determined to get this out. "I get that you're new to town, so let me give you some friendly advice. You can't go accusing people for no good reason. It won't go over well. You thought you had something with the notes you found in what you assumed is Victoria Masters's handwriting."

He raises a hand in the air to stop me. "I was right about the notes. Ms. Masters's sister is here in town. She was helping Victoria get settled in, and she confirmed it was her sister's handwriting on both papers."

Which means he's accusing me of lying when I said Samantha wrote them. And yeah, I was, but I'm not going to admit that. "She has very similar handwriting to the previous woman who leased the property then. What a coincidence."

"Yes, it is, isn't it?" His tone makes it evident he doesn't believe a word I'm saying.

"Did Victoria's sister have any idea what the notes meant?" I ask.

Detective Acosta smiles. Actually smiles. "See, this is what I meant before. I won't be sharing information with you or anyone else who isn't a member of the Bennett Falls Police Department. Do you understand that?"

I stand up. "Then I guess we're finished here, so if you don't mind, Cam and I will be getting back to our jobs. You know the coffee shop everyone in this town knows and loves." My words come out almost as a threat, but truth be told, the detective would be stupid to pick a fight with Cam and me. Our customers are like family to us. They'd come to our defense in a heartbeat. I've seen it before, and Detective Acosta won't stand a chance.

"Neither one of you should think of leaving town anytime soon," Detective Acosta says as we walk out of the interrogation room.

I pause and look over my shoulder. "This is our town, Detective. We're not going anywhere. You can count on that."

Mo bursts out laughing and slaps her open palm down on the table in Cup of Jo. "You threatened the new police detective!"

"I didn't *threaten* him, threaten him. I just told him how it is. There's a difference." I sip my mocha, wondering how bad I made things for myself by challenging Detective Acosta the way I did.

"I doubt he sees it that way," she says. "You called him out in front of the police department."

Cam rubs his hand up and down my back. "Luckily, there weren't many officers in the station at the time. "But I'm pretty sure I saw Officer Liberman crack a smile."

"Mo, Detective Acosta mentioned that Victoria Masters's sister is in town. Can you find out who she is and where she's staying? I'd like to talk to her."

"Of course, but aren't you worried that will get back

to Detective Acosta? I have a feeling he's going to be watching everything you do."

I'm getting the impression that Detective Acosta believes I was Quentin's downfall at the BFPD. Quentin's reputation took a bit of a hit thanks to me solving a few cases for him. I'm not sure if Detective Acosta is intimidated by me or if he doesn't want to deal with a civilian getting in his way.

"I'll handle Detective Acosta. Besides, he'll never solve this case if he spends all his time watching me."

Mo is on her phone. "Okay, it looks like Victoria Masters had two sisters, one older and one younger than she was. The older sister is Chloe Francis, and the younger sister is Hazel Francis."

"Neither changed their name?" Wes asks.

"I'm not sure. A lot of people use their maiden names on social media so previous classmates can find them. Victoria Masters uses Victoria Francis Masters for her online presence. That's how I found her sisters so quickly." Mo narrows her eyes at her phone screen. "It might take me a little while to get contact info and find out which sister is in town."

"Can I see their pictures?" I ask. There's a good chance the sister came into Cup of Jo since we're right next door to Victoria Masters's flower shop.

"Here." Mo turns her phone to me. "This is a photo of all three of them. Vicky is in the middle. Hazel is on the left of her, and Chloe is on the right."

Neither woman looks familiar to me, but Jamar,

Robin, or Tyler might have seen one of them. "Would you send me that photo so I can show it around?"

"You got it."

"We should get back to work before Mr. Kimball notices we're gone," Wes tells Mo as he stands up and offers her his hand.

"Ugh, you're right. Jo, I'll text you as soon as I have something."

"Thanks, Mo."

Once they leave, Cam heads back to the kitchen, and I show the photograph of the Francis sisters to Jamar.

He squints at the picture. "I think I might have seen this woman here." He points to Hazel, the younger sister. "She looks vaguely familiar."

"When do you think you might have seen her?"

"It was probably over the weekend, while you and Cam were away on your honeymoon."

That would make sense. Hazel and Victoria would have been setting up the flower shop.

Robin walks over to us with an empty pot of coffee. "What are we all looking at?"

"The victim's sisters," I say.

Robin places the pot back under the coffee machine and sets it to brew a new one. "For any reason in particular?"

"Yeah, Detective Acosta said one of her sisters was in town helping Victoria set up her new shop. I wanted to talk to the sister."

"Can I see the picture?" Robin asks.

I turn my phone to her. "Yeah, I've seen her before."

"The one on the left?" I ask.

"No, on the right. She lives in town."

Chloe Francis is a resident in Bennett Falls? I open my internet browser and search "Chloe Francis Bennett Falls, Pennsylvania." I nearly laugh when I find her address. "I've got it." Maybe Mo isn't the only Coffee sister with research skills after all.

Cam comes out of the kitchen and joins us. "You look happy," he tells me.

"I found an address for Chloe Francis right here in Bennett Falls."

Instead of being happy about it, Cam furrows his brow. "Didn't Detective Acosta say Victoria's sister was visiting from out of town?"

"He must be talking about the other sister then," Jamar says. "The one I recognized."

"You did?" Robin asks. "Let me see the photograph again."

I show it to her.

"Wait. Did she come in for a to-go order on Saturday when we were really busy?" Robin asks Jamar.

He snaps his fingers and points to her. "Yes! That was it."

"Wow, and you remembered her," I say to Jamar. "That's impressive."

"Yeah, I totally forgot about her," Robin says.

Jamar blushes. "She was wearing this shirt that looked identical to one Summer owns." Summer's

Jamar's girlfriend. They haven't been together for that long, but he's really into her.

"That makes more sense now," Robin says.

"This means we might be able to talk to both sisters and get some information," I say. "Thanks, guys."

"Happy to help," Jamar says, and Robin smiles.

Since I have an address for Chloe Francis, I decide to start there. Plus, there's a good chance Hazel is staying with her older sister since she's in town visiting. With Cup of Jo in more than capable hands, Cam and I leave to track down Chloe. I bring a box of Cam's pastries so we can talk to the Francis sisters under the guise of offering our condolences.

She lives in a cute little neighborhood I never even realized existed. I don't normally come over this way because it's on the opposite side of town. The neighborhood is off a back road, and I honestly thought it was all just woods back here.

Cam parks in the driveway behind a white Audi and blue Mustang. "It certainly seems like someone is home."

Since her sister is visiting, I'd think Chloe would have planned for a little time off from work. She could have been helping Victoria get settled as well.

We knock on the door, and a dog barks inside.

"Baxter, hush!" a woman's voice says as the door opens. She looks at us and says, "Can I help you?" I recognize her from the photograph. She's the older sister, Chloe.

"Hi, I'm Camden Turner, and this is my wife, Joanna Coffee. We own Cup of Jo on Main Street."

"Hello," she says.

I hold out the box of pastries. "We wanted to offer our sincerest condolences," I say. "Your sister's flower shop was right next door to ours, but I'm afraid we never got to meet because Cam and I were away on our honeymoon."

She takes the box. "Oh, well, thank you. I've been to your coffee shop. Whichever one of you bakes, you're extremely talented."

"That would be me," Cam says. "Thank you."

"Ms. Francis, do you think we could speak to you for a moment. I promise we won't stay long," I say.

"What about?" she asks, still not budging from her place in the doorway.

"Well, as it turns out, your sister wrote my name on a piece of paper, and I can't for the life of me figure out why."

"Who's at the door?" another woman asks.

Chloe makes no move to answer her. "Come in."

We step into the house, which looks like Chloe either hired an interior designer to decorate or maybe she is one.

"Your home is beautiful," I say.

"Thank you. If you ever need a decorator, I'm your girl. I run my own business."

"Chloe, who..." Hazel walks into the entryway. "Friends of yours?" she asks her sister.

"Not exactly. These people own the café on Main Street next to…" Chloe stops abruptly and wipes a tear from her eye.

Hazel rushes to her older sister and hugs her, tears now falling from her eyes as well. I feel awful for intruding on them like this when they're clearly grieving.

"We're so sorry for your loss," I tell Hazel.

Hazel pulls away from her sister and wipes her cheeks. "Thank you. I still can't believe she's gone. It doesn't make sense to me."

"We don't want to keep you. We were hoping you could answer a quick question for us."

"The note with your name on it," Chloe says. "I think I'm to blame for that. Victoria wanted to have a grand opening, complete with food and drinks. I suggested she contact you because I love your baked goods. I didn't know your names, though, only the name of your café. I'm guessing Victoria looked up your website and wrote down your name so she could talk to you in person about catering for her grand opening."

"She had this thing about calling people by name," Hazel says. "She's a people person. Or…she was." Hazel starts crying again. "Excuse me." She turns and walks toward the kitchen, which is visible from the entryway.

"I wonder what the second note meant," Cam said. "The one that read 'mocha.'"

"I know what that was about, too," Chloe says. "I suggested she paint the place mocha. I had given her some paint samples, and I thought that color would really brighten up the place while also offering a little warmth."

Flashing lights illuminate the room, and Cam looks out the front door. "Is that—"

"Detective Acosta," I say, knowing we've been caught.

CHAPTER SIX

With Detective Acosta's patrol car blocking Cam's SUV in the driveway, there's no chance of us getting out of here without being seen.

"What is he doing back here?" Chloe asks.

"He's been here before?" I ask.

"Yes, he knows Victoria was staying with me while her house was being built."

Detective Acosta is out of his patrol car now and approaching the front door. He pauses at Cam's SUV and writes down the license plate number. I'm sure it's all for show because I'm convinced he's already looked it up to check the toll into New Jersey and confirm we were there yesterday.

"He doesn't look happy," Chloe says.

"I don't think he ever looks happy." I turn for the door. "We should go. We just wanted to bring you those pastries and tell you how sorry we are for your loss." I open the door before Detective Acosta can.

"Ms. Coffee, Mr. Turner, how funny that I should find you here."

"I'm not sure what's funny about it, but we were leaving and you're blocking our car," I say.

Detective Acosta turns around to look. "Yes, I suppose I am."

"Great, could you move your vehicle?"

Cam places his hand on my back, silently communicating that I should ease up. Attacking Detective Acosta probably isn't in my best interest, but I'm conditioned not to hold back after dealing with Quentin for so long.

"We'd appreciate it," Cam adds. "We need to get back to work. We were delivering some pastries to Ms. Francis."

"Is that right? You deliver now?" Detective Acosta asks with a smug look on his face.

"Not exactly. We were offering our condolences. We might not have gotten to meet Victoria, but her sister is a fellow resident of Bennett Falls, and as I told you, we're a close-knit town." Except I didn't even know Chloe Francis until about ten minutes ago.

"I see. Well, isn't that nice of you?"

I need to do something to get this man off my back. I turn to Chloe and say, "Are you still planning to paint the flower shop mocha? I'm just curious because if you already bought the mocha paint and no longer plan to use it for the flower shop, I'd be happy to buy it from you.

My parents own a coffee shop as well, and my mother loves that particular paint color."

"Oh, I don't think Vicky actually bought the paint yet," Chloe says.

"I see. Well, I appreciate that you recommended Cup of Jo to her for catering. It was very sweet of you. I hope you enjoy the pastries, and please stop in anytime."

Detective Acosta narrows his eyes at me.

"Detective, your car," I say, gesturing to it.

"Give me one moment," he tells Chloe before he turns back to his patrol car. I have no doubt he'll follow up with her about the sticky notes. It must have been Hazel he asked about them before. She must not have known why Vicky wrote my name and mocha on the pieces of paper. At least this is one part of the mystery solved, and maybe now he'll stop questioning me so much.

He doesn't say a word to Cam and me as he gets into his patrol car and backs out of the driveway. I'm tempted to wave to him as we pull away, but I tuck my hands under my legs to keep myself under control.

"Are you going to be okay?" Cam asks, turning his head to look at me briefly.

"Yeah, but it feels like Acosta is out to get me. Like he's made it his personal mission to take me down since he thinks I'm the reason Quentin left the BFPD."

"Quentin leaving Bennett Falls had nothing to do with you."

Maybe it did a little. This was always his town, but

after our breakup—which was totally his fault—everyone turned on him. He lost the respect of the other residents. Add in his son's premature birth and me showing him up a few times with his investigations, and it was all too much for him to deal with. He's better off somewhere else, and yeah, I'm a big part of that.

"Hey." Cam reaches over and squeezes my hand. "I can tell you're feeling at least partly responsible for this, but that's absurd. Quentin had to face the consequences of his actions. He put himself in that position. You didn't do anything wrong."

Maybe, but Quentin also told me he always knew I loved Cam. Apparently, everyone in town knew that before I did. Quentin might have cheated on me, but he also thought I never really loved him, and maybe he's right about that.

"Detective Acosta is going to figure out that messing with us isn't a good idea," Cam says. "If he chooses to be stupid about it and ruin his reputation in town before this case is finished, that's on him."

"I know." I give a small laugh. "Mrs. Marlow could take him down in seconds."

Cam laughs. "Yeah, she could. He should watch out for her."

Back at Cup of Jo, Cam and I have a quick bite to eat. I'm not sure I've eaten any real meals besides dinners. My breakfasts and lunches have consisted of baked goods. I'm lucky I have a decent metabolism. Of course, the excessive amounts of coffee I drink might have something to do with that. Can caffeine boost your metabolism? It certainly makes me feel like I'm running around all the time.

"At least we figured out what the notes mean," Cam says.

"I'm still leaning toward the ex-husband as the killer."

Robin walks over to the table. "Are the police sure this was murder?"

"Actually, no. Detective Acosta is the one who is convinced there was foul play. Why do you ask?"

"Well, it seems to me like she could have slipped. Crazy accidents happen, right? And if she was carrying things and couldn't see the steps, I could see her falling."

She's right. We don't even know what Vicky was wearing when she fell. Was she in sneakers, flip-flops, sandals? Was she carrying boxes from the storage area above the flower shop? If Quentin were here, I'd know these details. But Detective Acosta has kept all this information locked up tight.

"We need to talk to someone who was at the crime scene," I say.

"How do you plan to do that?" Cam asks. "Acosta will never tell us anything, and as much as I think Officer Liberman is the friendliest face at the BFPD, I don't believe he'll give us that kind of information either."

That leaves two people who might know something. Two people I don't want to bother because they're already hurting. "We might have to ask Vicky's sisters."

"We can't show up there again, Jo." Cam looks out the front windows. "I'm surprised Acosta's patrol car isn't parked out front. He's clearly keeping a close eye on us."

"Maybe not anymore. Chloe explained why my name and the word mocha were on those notes. I'd say that clears suspicion."

"I'd say so, too, but does Detective Acosta think so?" Cam asks.

Probably not. "He has to be looking into the ex-husband, though."

"And looking into why we went to see the ex-husband."

"Okay, but we never actually talked to Thomas Masters, so he can't prove that's what we did. He can only prove we were in New Jersey."

"And that we spoke to Cheryl Ziegler and Grace Marsh," Cam reminds me. "If he asks them directly if they spoke to us, I doubt they'd lie. He is an officer of the law, and they don't know us well enough to want to cover for us."

No, they don't. I can't worry about Detective Acosta following up with Victoria Masters's old neighbors, though. I need to focus on figuring out how she died. If I can solve this case, it might get Detective Acosta off my back. Or it might make him even angrier with me. "I might have to solve this and then lead Acosta to the answer without him realizing it," I say.

"You might be right."

The first thing I need is to see the crime scene. Detective Acosta might not be willing to let me into the flower shop, but I now know someone else who might. "I need to call Chloe Francis."

"Why?"

"Because she and Hazel must have keys to the flower shop."

"Why would they agree to let us in there?" Cam asks, finishing his apple strudel and pushing his plate aside.

"I can offer to help clear out the space. I doubt either sister wants to go back there since it's where Vicky died."

"I guess it's worth a shot."

I look around at all the customers inside Cup of Jo. I shouldn't make the call here. Someone might overhear me, and the last thing I need is rumors circulating around town that I'm investigating this case. "Let's go into the kitchen."

We clear our plates and mugs before heading into the kitchen for some privacy to make the call. I text Mo to see if she found the contact information for the sisters yet since all I came up with was Chloe's address.

My phone rings in response. "Hi, Mo."

"Hey, so I have the number of Chloe Francis's interior design business."

"Great. Cam and I found her home address and went to see her, but Detective Acosta showed up and cut the visit short. I need to call her."

"Uh-oh. What happened with Acosta?"

"Well, words were exchanged."

She laughs. "I'm sure they were. Be careful, Jo. He's

not Quentin. And I can't help thinking part of you is sad about that."

"I'm not sad he's gone. It's just strange."

"I know. This town is weird that way. We've grown used to dealing with people we don't like. Everyone has their place, and when that place is vacated, it leaves this empty feeling."

Sometimes Mo can be mature beyond her years. "You miss insulting him, don't you?"

"I really do. It fulfilled this weird need I have for being sarcastic and maybe even a little vengeful."

"It makes me feel better that you feel that way."

"Still, it's nice not to have to see his face. My fist had a way of wanting to connect with his nose."

I laugh. "I think a lot of people would agree with you there. But if he ever comes back and that opportunity arises, I'm first in line."

"Rightfully so. I'm texting you Chloe's business number now. I have a meeting to get to."

"Thanks, Mo." I end the call and open my messages to retrieve her text.

Cam's been cleaning the kitchen, but now that I'm off with Mo, he puts down the dish towel and leans against the island next to me.

I dial Chloe's number.

"Francis Interior Design, this is Chloe. How can I help you?"

"Chloe, it's Joanna Coffee from Cup of Jo."

"Oh. Hello." The forced cheerfulness she used to

answer the call disappears now that she knows I'm not a potential client calling to hire her.

"Hi, I'm sorry for rushing out earlier."

"I got the impression you and the detective don't get along very well. Are you exes or something?"

"No." That would be me and the former police detective. "He questioned me earlier about my name on that note."

"Oh, that makes sense. I hope he didn't suspect you of anything. You didn't even know my sister."

"He did, but I'm hoping your explanation got him off that trail. Chloe, I hate to ask you this, but do you think your sister's fall was just an unfortunate accident, or do you think someone might have pushed her?"

She sighs loudly into the phone. "I don't know. Vicky's ex-husband could have done this for sure. He's hurt her in the past, but as far as I know, he has no idea she's in Bennett Falls. I mean, he didn't know she was." She sighs heavily into the phone. "It so hard to accept she's really gone. I keep talking about her as if she's still here."

That's understandable. "Is there anything I can do for you and Hazel?"

"I don't think so. We're just trying to get through making all the arrangements. Our parents passed away two years ago, so we only have each other. The services will be small."

"What about the flower shop?"

"We have to clear it out."

"I know the previous renter, the original owner of Bouquets of Love. I could call her and see if she'd like to buy the flowers or anything else from you so you don't have to worry about getting rid of them."

"Thanks, but we've decided to have a sidewalk sale. The police said it would be okay since..." She takes a deep breath. "Since Vicky died in the back by the staircase. That part is blocked off, so we have to keep everyone out front."

"Is there anything Cam and I can do to help?" I ask.

"We'd love the help if you're serious about it," Chloe says.

"Absolutely. Just tell us what you need."

"Thank you. This has really been hard on Hazel. She's the one who found Vicky. She spends all her time in the bedroom, crying. I've never seen her like this. She and Vicky were really close, though. I'm ten years older than Hazel, so I was off at college by the time she was eight. We didn't bond the way Hazel and Vicky did."

"Well, Cam and I are available to help you both whenever you need. When were you planning to have the sidewalk sale?"

"As soon as possible. We don't want the flowers to die before we can sell them. Vicky didn't have much life insurance, and all her money was going toward building her new house. We don't have much to work with."

"Do you want to meet me this afternoon? Cam and I can get started right away."

"Thank you. That would be a big help. I'll send

Hazel to meet you because I have a client appointment I need to get to very soon."

"That works for us. Tell Hazel to come any time. We'll be ready."

I hang up and meet Cam's gaze. "Well, looks like we'll be seeing the crime scene today."

CHAPTER SEVEN

Hazel shows up at Cup of Jo a little before closing. Thankfully, Jamar and Robin are very skilled at running every aspect of this place, so Cam and I go next door with Hazel.

Her hand shakes as she unlocks the door. "I don't know if I can do this. The last time I was here was when…"

I reach for her hand. "You don't have to go inside. If you're comfortable leaving the keys with Cam and me, we'll take care of this for you."

"You're both so nice to help us like this." She hands the keys to me. "The bigger one is for the front door and back door. The smaller one is for the storage room upstairs, but I don't think it's locked."

"What do you need us to do?" Cam asks.

"All the boxes upstairs need to be brought down, but…" Tears stream down her cheeks.

Bringing the boxes down means walking down the stairs where her sister died. "Chloe said the police blocked off that area," I say.

"They know we have to get the boxes upstairs. They just don't want any customers back there. We were told the forensics team already went over everything."

"Okay, we'll handle it then."

"Chloe is making signs for the sidewalk sale tomorrow. We'll bring out the flowers in the morning. Chloe is bringing tables to put them all on." Hazel looks like she's moments from collapsing.

"Go home, Hazel. We'll handle things here," I tell her.

She sniffles and heads back to her car.

I look around to make sure Detective Acosta isn't lurking somewhere nearby, watching us. The coast seems to be clear, though. Maybe Chloe's explanation of the two notes cleared my name after all.

I open the door and step inside. The place still looks the way Samantha left it. The refrigerated case is full of flowers, and there are arrangements displayed throughout the space. I know the stairs are in the back behind the counter and register. Cam and I walk back there. There's no actual police tape since the space isn't currently being used by anyone, but there is evidence that the forensics team came through. There are markers on the ground to show where Vicky's body was discovered at the bottom of the stairs. As far as crime scenes go, this one is pretty mild. Vicky died from a broken neck, so there's no blood splatter or anything like that.

"These stairs are steep," Cam says. "I can see how it would be easy to fall down them, especially if Vicky was carrying a box and couldn't see the steps as she walked."

I look around for a box on the ground but don't see one. It's possible the forensics team took it, though.

We start up the stairs, careful not to touch the railing. I don't want my fingerprints on anything. Detective Acosta would have a field day with that. When we get to the top of the stairs, we see the door to the storage area is open. Hot air pours out of the room toward us.

"I guess they haven't been running the air conditioning or fan up here," Cam says.

"Yeah, apparently not. It's like a sauna up here." I grab the front of my shirt and pull it away from my body. "Do you see a thermostat anywhere?"

"I'm not sure we should turn on the air conditioning if we find a thermostat. We don't want anyone to know we were here."

"Chloe or Hazel could easily mention we were helping them," I say. "It does give us a good reason for being here."

"I guess that's true. It's also probably not good for the flowers downstairs if this hot air messes with the temperature in the shop itself. I wonder why this door was left open to begin with."

"They must have found it open when they discovered Vicky's body. And if she left it open, it could mean her hands were full, and she couldn't close the door behind her before she went down the stairs."

"Meaning her death was most likely an accident," Cam says.

"It very well might have been." Detective Acosta could be making more out of this than there actually is. I could see him wanting to make a name for himself on his very first case and that motivating him to see something that isn't really there.

"How do we prove it was only an accident, though?" Cam asks.

Normally, I'd say it's Detective Acosta's job to prove it wasn't an accident. He's the one who needs evidence, not us. But something tells me Detective Acosta knows a lot about my involvement in Quentin's cases, and he's determined to one-up me from the start. He's going to come up with something to prove this wasn't an accident. And if there really is evidence to show this wasn't an accident, I have to find it before he does.

Cam and I move several boxes downstairs. We take our time on the stairs because they are really steep, and neither one of us wants to end up like Vicky. Most of the things are left over from Samantha's business. Glass vases, ribbon, tiny cards with envelopes, and those plastic card holders that go in bouquets. Other than the vases, nothing is heavy, which makes me wonder if Vicky tried to stack the lighter boxes and totally obstructed her view of the stairs.

Once we're finished upstairs, we go back to the

counter. There's a filing cabinet underneath it that I never noticed before. Samantha didn't strike me as the type to keep records of things. She wasn't exactly the most organized person. I reach for the filing cabinet, but Cam stops me.

"What are you doing?"

"I don't think this belonged to Samantha. I think it was Vicky's."

"We can't just go through it," he says.

"Why not? I'm sure the police already have, and it's not like Vicky will be using it anymore. If it helps us figure out if someone wanted to kill her, I think we need to go through it." As much as I think this could have been an accident, I don't want to let someone get away with murdering Vicky if it wasn't. I'm not saying I believe in ghosts or anything, but I wouldn't like the idea of someone getting away with killing me if I were in Vicky's position.

"Okay, but we should be wearing gloves. I don't want our fingerprints on the filing cabinet since there's no reason we should be looking in there when we aren't supposed to be investigating Vicky's death in the first place."

I can't argue with that logic, so I look around for gloves. Samantha Perry was the type of woman to always have her nails painted and perfectly filed. She most likely wore gloves when working with the flowers, so there has to be a box of latex gloves around here somewhere. I bend down to see under the counter.

There's a small door, indicating a storage area. I grab one of the plastic card holders from a nearby box and slide it under the handle on the door. Then I pull it open.

Bingo. Samantha has spray bottles and boxes of gloves under here. I reach for the open box of gloves and pull out four, handing two to Cam. If Detective Acosta were to show up right now, we'd probably both we hauled out of here in handcuffs. We couldn't look guiltier of snooping at the moment.

After slipping on the gloves, I open the filing cabinet. As I suspected, it's Vicky's. She has labeled folders for "Orders to be Completed," "Fulfilled Orders," "Canceled Orders," "Blank Order Forms," "Supply Budget," "Expenses," and a few others. Everything looks pretty standard for someone starting up a business.

I'm about to close the drawer when I realize there's a folder in the back with papers in it but no label on the tab. I pull it out and open the folder. "It's a restraining order against Thomas Masters," I say, scanning the document.

"Mo said that was dropped, didn't she?" Cam asks, standing beside me to read the papers himself.

"Yeah, but it looks like Vicky kept a copy."

"Maybe she was afraid she'd have to use it after all. You know, if Thomas found her here in Bennett Falls."

That makes a lot of sense. Vicky seems like she was the type of person to prepare for everything. At least that's the impression I'm getting from the files she kept.

But then again, it's possible she owned a flower shop before and already knew what she would need here.

"Another possibility is that Thomas already found her here," Cam says.

I wag a finger at him. "Yes, and if he did, she might have gotten the process for the restraining order rolling again. If he found out, he might have come here to confront her. They fought, and he pushed her down the stairs."

"You think Thomas killed my sister?" Hazel asks, walking up behind us.

I whirl around, my hand to my chest. "Hazel, you scared me. I didn't hear you come in."

"Sorry, but the back door was unlocked."

It was? Cam and I didn't unlock it. Maybe the killer left through the back door. Or maybe someone has been here since Vicky's body was discovered.

"You don't have to apologize," Cam says. "You have more right to be here than we do."

"I wanted to see how you were doing, and I realized I need to face this…" She looks around the space.

I put the file folder with the restraining order on the counter. I want to ask Hazel about it, but this clearly isn't the time. She seems like she's on the verge of another breakdown. "It's only been a few days. Don't push your-self if you're not ready for this. No one expects you to get over your sister's death in two days." I reach for her and squeeze her arm.

"You guys are really nice. I just wish I knew what to

do. Chloe compartmentalizes everything and goes right into action with the funeral arrangements, calling the banks, everything." Hazel holds her arms out at her sides. "Then there's me. I feel like a stupid kid. I'm twenty-five, but right now I feel like I'm only fifteen. I'm clueless, and every time I think about Vicky, I break down and cry." She starts sobbing, and I wrap my arm around her shoulders.

"Hey, don't be so hard on yourself. You clearly loved your sister. If you ask me, that's the most important thing. Not how well you handle making arrangements now."

"Jo is right," Cam says in a soothing voice. "You and Vicky were close. You were there for her when it mattered."

"I just hope she knew how much I loved her."

"I'm sure she did." I rub Hazel's back. "Do you want us to drive you back to Chloe's house? I think you should try to get some rest. Vicky would want you to."

"No, I can drive myself. Driving helps clear my mind." She raises her head, her mascara streaking down both cheeks.

"We can come by later with some coffee and desserts if you'd like."

"You're really sweet, but you don't need to do that. I have Chloe. We'll be okay."

I nod.

"You're still going to be here for the sidewalk sale tomorrow, though, right?"

"Of course. We wouldn't miss it."

"I'll walk you to your car," Cam tells Hazel.

"Thank you."

I can't help feeling awful for Hazel. She's really taking her sister's death hard. I return the folder with the restraining order to the filing cabinet and close it. Thankfully, Hazel was too upset to care that Cam and I were snooping around. Still, we need to find out more about this restraining order and Thomas Masters.

Later that night, after dinner with Mo and Wes, we all take our coffees to the living room to do some more research. Jamar and Robin both have dates tonight, so it's only the four of us.

"The restraining order definitely didn't go through," Mo says.

"Do I even want to know what database you hacked your way into?" I ask.

"No. You really don't."

"Aren't you afraid someone will discover you hacked into it?" Cam asks. "I've seen shows where the cops trace the IP address back to the hacker."

"Let's just say I've taken precautions, and leave it at that."

I'm pretty sure Mo could have been arrested multiple times by now. If she wanted a career change, she could easily have a job working for law enforcement or maybe even the CIA. She finds things much faster than the IT department at the BFPD. I don't really see her getting along with Chief Harvey, though. She'd slip and call him a name that would have her handcuffed before her first day was done. I have to wonder how much Quentin covered for Mo as well as for me.

"We definitely need to find Thomas Masters and talk to him directly," I say.

"He won't like you asking questions," Wes says, sipping his coffee. "And if he calls the station to complain about you, you know Detective Acosta will be more than happy to charge you with interfering with his case."

The restraining order is the only lead we have so far, and it lines up perfectly with what Vicky's old neighbors told us about her bruises. Thomas Masters had a history of hurting his wife. I have no doubt in my mind he wouldn't hesitate to hurt his ex-wife, especially since she was threatening him with a restraining order. He probably saw it as his chance to hurt her one last time before she filed the restraining order. It might have even been the catalyst that prompted him to kill her.

"You want to go back to Columbia to talk to Thomas Masters?" Jamar asks me Thursday morning.

"It's our only lead. That restraining order might be the evidence we need." I look around at the crowd in Cup of Jo. "I can call Tyler in to help you and Robin here."

"I'm not worried about things here. I'm worried about you and Cam." Jamar finishes making Mrs.

Marlow's cappuccino and hands it to her. "On me. I pay my debts."

"Debts?" I ask.

"We made a bet," Mrs. Marlow says, winking at Jamar.

"You got lucky." Jamar frowns.

"Wait. What did you two bet on?" I ask, my gaze volleying between them.

"Whether or not the new police detective would be questioning you on his first case."

"I can't believe you two bet on that." I cross my arms, which loses some effect since I'm holding a dish rag I just used to clean the counter.

"Come on, Jo," Mrs. Marlow said. "It was an easy bet to make. You do have a certain knack for getting involved in cases."

"Because I try to help the people in this town."

She reaches forward and pats my arm. "I never said it was a bad thing. You're a good girl, Joanna Coffee. You always have been, and the citizens of Bennett Falls are lucky to have you on their side."

"Thank you."

She smiles and walks back to her table with her drink. I turn to glare at Jamar. "You bet I wouldn't get involved in this case?"

"I thought with Quentin gone you'd focus on running this place."

I thought so, too. "What are the odds that a woman would die in the store next to Cup of Jo?"

"With you, very good. You're kind of a magnet for…" He pauses.

"If you say murders, I'm docking your pay." I wag a finger in front of him.

He laughs. "No, I was going to say mysteries. You solved Quentin's cases a whole lot faster than he did. I'm sure it will be no different with this new detective."

I'm not so sure. "You know, if Detective Acosta wasn't pursuing the murder angle, I don't think I would have even considered it. This would be ruled an accident, and I'd be staying here all day serving coffee."

"You think he's on to something, though, don't you?"

"I'm not sure. He might be trying to prove something since he's new to the BFPD. But maybe he's following his gut. For all we know, he might be a great detective."

"With a chip on his shoulder," Jamar says.

"We know nothing about where he came from and why he left to come here." I'm going to have to ask Mo to dig up some dirt on the new detective. "Hang on." I quickly text Mo and ask her to do just that. Know your enemy, right? If that's what he's going to be. That much is still to be determined.

When I'm finished, I look at Jamar. "Do you think I'm crazy for getting involved in this case?"

"Actually, I'd think something was wrong with you if you didn't. It's not in your nature to look the other way when something bad happens."

"Then why did you bet Mrs. Marlow I'd stay out of this?" I ask.

He smiles. "She's a great customer and a great person. I didn't mind losing to her or having to buy her coffee." So he was only pretending to be upset he lost the bet.

I smile at him. "Now that I can understand."

"Hey," Cam says, coming out of the kitchen. "I saw Detective Acosta driving around the back of the café. I think he's staking out the place."

"Maybe he's staking out the flower shop," Jamar says. "That is the murder scene, right?"

"I suppose." Cam doesn't look convinced.

"He might know someone was in the flower shop yesterday," I say.

"What time is the sidewalk sale?" he asks. "I haven't seen any sign of Chloe or Hazel Francis, but I thought they said they were doing it today."

He's right. I haven't seen either of them. "They didn't give me a specific time. They only said it was this morning."

"Maybe they had to postpone," Jamar suggests.

Mickey comes running up to the counter. "Jo, Cam, did you hear?"

"Here what?"

"Someone broke into the flower shop late last night. The police are there now with the dead lady's older sister."

I turn to Cam. "Why would someone break in there? There's nothing to steal but some flowers."

"Let's go talk to Chloe and find out," he says.

We hurry out the front of Cup of Jo. The police are there, but they're being discreet about it since the flower shop isn't open for customers anyway. Chloe comes walking out, and I wave as soon as she sees us.

"You two didn't see anything, did you?" she asks us. "There's a broken window out back, and the door was wide open this morning. They're checking for prints."

I rack my brain, trying to remember what Cam and I touched before we put on gloves. This could go downhill really quickly. Especially since the BFPD has both our prints on file.

CHAPTER EIGHT

I try not to panic. Hazel let us in, and she'll vouch for our presence. I have to stay calm so we don't look guilty of anything.

"Chloe, was anything taken?" I ask.

"The filing cabinet was wide open. I don't know if anything was missing because I have no idea what was in there. It was Vicky's, and I never looked inside it."

I turn to Cam. Do we tell her? She'll probably tell Detective Acosta, and then we'll be brought in for questioning. "Were there any files in there?" I ask. "Did you see?"

"They were all empty. Some were labeled, but I don't know if they ever contained paperwork or not."

"They were *all* empty?" I ask.

"Yeah, why?" She narrows her eyes at me.

"Well, we were there yesterday, helping Hazel bring some boxes down from the upstairs storage room."

"What does that have to do with my sister's filing cabinet?" she asks.

I have to think quickly. "I was going to leave a note for Hazel. She's been so upset about Vicky, and I didn't want to bother her in person. I was looking for some paper and a pen. I thought there might be paper in the filing cabinet."

"Was there?" Chloe asks.

"Yes."

"Did you see what was on it?" I can tell she's getting frustrated that she has to pry this out of me.

"It was a restraining order against Thomas Masters," I say in a low voice.

"Say that again," comes Detective Acosta's voice from directly behind me.

I turn around to face him. "Good morning, Detective."

"What's this about a restraining order?"

"We accidentally found one in the filing cabinet yesterday when we were helping Hazel clear out some things for the sidewalk sale today."

"The sale." Chloe slams her fist against the side of her leg. "Well, I guess that's off. What am I going to do with all these flowers now?"

"You can bring them next door in front of Cup of Jo," Cam says. "We can sell them for you."

"Really?" Chloe looks at me, and I nod. Then she raises her gaze to Detective Acosta. "Can we bring the flowers out?"

"After we're finished taking prints and searching the place, you can remove the flowers, but only the flowers."

"Thank you." Chloe looks relieved. "I'll call Hazel. I don't know where she is. She should be here by now." She takes her phone from her back pocket and walks a few feet away to make her call.

"What time were you here yesterday?" Detective Acosta asks us.

"Sometime in the afternoon," Cam says.

"All we did was carry some boxes downstairs," I say before I realize that's going to be a problem for Detective Acosta.

"You carried them down the stairs where Victoria Masters was killed?" he asks, his tone conveying how displeased he is by that.

"We were only trying to help Hazel," I say.

"That area is still off-limits. Do you realize you tampered with a crime scene?"

"I'm sorry, but Hazel was going to do it herself, and she's been really upset over her sister's death. We weren't trying to mess up your investigation." I need to get his focus on something more important to the case. "But we did see a restraining order in that filing cabinet. If it's not there now, then that's what was taken last night when someone broke in."

Chloe turns back to us. "Hazel is almost here. She got a flat tire this morning. I swear it's been one thing after another. We can't seem to catch a break lately." Chloe looks like she's going to scream or cry. I can't tell which, and I'm not sure she's decided on one over the other either.

"What did you touch when you were in there?" Detective Acosta asks Cam and me.

"A lot of things," I say. "The boxes, the door upstairs, the counter downstairs, the filing cabinet, when we were looking for paper to write Hazel a note." I want to give him a long list so he doesn't question us later.

Detective Acosta doesn't look the least bit happy. "I have your prints on file, so it won't be a problem to check them."

The question is why does he know our prints are on file? "Detective, Thomas Masters is the only person who would want that restraining order."

"What makes you think he'd want it?" he asks.

Seriously? I thought this guy was smarter than Quentin, but it seems like I'm going to have to spell this out for him. "If Victoria had a reason to take out a restraining order on him, that makes him a suspect."

"Not necessarily."

"He physically hurt her. She had bruises on her arms from him."

Detective Acosta crosses his arms. "How would you know that, Ms. Coffee?"

"How don't you know that, *Detective*?" I stress the word "detective" so he's aware I'm questioning is ability to do his job.

Cam wraps an arm around me. "You wanted to know

if we were in Columbia the other day, and the answer is yes. We were."

I turn to Cam, questioning why on earth he'd tell the detective that.

"Jo, if we don't come clean with him, it's only going to make him suspect us."

Chloe narrows her eyes at Detective Acosta. "Why would you suspect two people who weren't in town and never even met my sister?"

I won't lie. The expression on Detective Acosta's face right now is priceless.

"I'm questioning everyone. These two rent the space next to this one. They and their employees have perfect access to it, and no one would question them since they work so close by."

"But they have no reason to kill a perfect stranger." Chloe throws her hands in the air. "You know I'm starting to think this was an accident and none of this is necessary. You're putting us through torture for no reason at all. What kind of monster are you?"

I was wrong earlier. Whether Chloe would scream or cry wasn't an either-or situation. She's doing both right now. I move toward her to console her, and Hazel pulls up, a spare tire on the front driver's side. She looks panicked when she gets out and sees Chloe so upset.

"What's going on?" Hazel asks.

"Nothing," Chloe says. "Let's go home. I'm finished with the detective and his theories. Our sister had an accident. It was awful, yes, but that's what happened."

She loops her arm through Hazel's. "Come on. You can drive home with me. I'll call the mechanic across the street to get you a new tire."

We watch them walk away before turning back to Detective Acosta.

"Why do you always stick your nose in the BFPD's investigations?" he asks me. "I know about your prior connection to Detective Perry, but he's gone. You need to let this go, Ms. Coffee."

"Are you going to let this go?" I ask. "Chloe seems convinced her sister's death was an accident."

He finally lowers his arms to his sides. "Do you think someone would break in here and steal something if they weren't responsible for Victoria Masters's murder?"

No, I don't. I'll give him that. I discreetly shake my head. "Like I said, Thomas Masters seems to want to keep that restraining order a secret."

"I'm going to warn you once to stay away from my investigation. The next time I catch you snooping around where you shouldn't be, whether it's here or in New Jersey, I will arrest you both for interference." He looks from me to Cam before saying, "Now, I have work to do." He walks back into the flower shop.

He might think he's won, but Chloe gave us permission to sell the flowers in front of Cup of Jo today after the police finish up inside Bouquets of Love. That means we have permission to go back inside and see if there's anything Detective Acosta and his team missed.

When we turn back toward Cup of Jo, the windows

are filled with faces. Mickey Baldwin is front and center, but I'd expect no less from him.

We walk inside, and everyone scrambles back to their seats. It's comical how they all pretend to be in conversations about other things. I walk over and sit down beside Mickey, who is talking about the weather.

"Chance of showers later. I'm not sure we'll get it, though. The skies look pretty clear to me." He looks past me out the front windows as if checking the sky for himself to confirm.

"The weather, Mickey? Really? Come on. I expect better from you." I shake my head and stand up.

"Aw, come on, Jo. Throw us a bone here. What happened? You all looked pretty heated."

"Let's just say the new detective doesn't seem to like me anymore than the last one did."

"Did you break his heart, too?" Mrs. Marlow asks me.

"I never broke Quentin's heart. He used me to get closer to Samantha."

Cam loops an arm around my waist. "He was an idiot, but I think it worked out well in the end."

I look up at him and smile. "It definitely did." I couldn't be happier to be married to Cam. You can't even compare Quentin to him. The hardest part of my breakup with Quentin, the part that still bothers me today, is that two people I thought cared about me betrayed me. I lost two friends. That's what really hurt.

"Maybe Detective Acosta is just upset you're off the market, Jo," Mrs. Marlow says.

"I don't think that's what it is," I say.

Mo rushes into Cup of Jo. "I saw everything from my office window. I would have been here sooner, but the stupid elevator got stuck." She reaches for my arm. "Are you okay?"

"I'm fine. Bouquets of Love was broken into, and the detective was asking questions because Cam and I were moving boxes for the Francis sisters yesterday. Our prints are in there, so the detective needed to know what we touched."

"Oh, so they can rule you two out as suspects," Mickey says. "That's actually good news, Jo."

Yeah, if I thought that was what Detective Acosta was really doing. If he doesn't follow the lead I gave him, I'll know he's out to get me personally. What I won't know is why.

"Mo, did you look into what I asked you to look into?" I don't want to come out and say it in front of the crowd.

"I was in the middle of that when I saw the commotion outside on the sidewalk."

"Okay, can you get back to it as soon as possible?"

"Caffeine me, and I'll go do it now," she says.

I smile and motion for her to follow me to the counter. "What do you want?"

"How about two mochas? They were really good. I can't seem to get enough of them."

"You got it."

I make her drinks and put a chocolate straw in each. "Tell Wes I said hi, and if he wants to buy you some flowers, we'll be selling the bouquets from next door later today. We're just waiting for the police to clear out first."

"I do like flowers," she says as she takes the cups.

The police finish up next door around midday. Chloe comes back to help us move the flowers. She's ready to be done with all of this. That much is clear.

We get the floral arrangements set up on tables outside Cup of Jo, and I change the special board to read "Free cup of coffee with every flower purchase." Robin brings the coffee urn outside along with the small to-go cups. The event draws a crowd. I think most people just want to gossip about the possible murder, but we're selling the flowers, which helps Chloe and Hazel.

Mo comes from across the street around two o'clock with Wes in tow. "The setup looks great, and it seems like you've already sold quite a bit."

"Thanks. We have," I tell her. Robin and I have been handling the sidewalk sale while Cam and Jamar take care of things inside. Tyler was feeling a little under the weather this morning, so I told him to take a few days off to recover.

"Jo, I found something pretty big on Detective Acosta," Mo says, lowering her voice.

"What?"

She motions for us to go inside, not wanting to talk in front of the crowd. I hate leaving Robin alone out here, so I motion for Mo to follow me. "Jamar, I need you to help Robin outside for a few minutes," I say.

"No problem." He spins one of the customers he was dancing with before heading outside.

"He's quite the showman," Mo says, following me into the kitchen.

"That he is. The customers love his dancing, though, so I don't think he'll ever stop."

"Hey, Mo," Cam says with a big smile as we enter his space. "What's my new sister-in-law up to today?"

"Digging up dirt on a certain police detective."

"What did you find out?" I ask, trying not to sound as eager as I am to hear this.

"Turns out that Detective Acosta was only recently promoted to detective. He worked in L.A. before he moved here. His first case as a detective didn't go well. He was the lead on the case, and he ruled it an accident."

This is sounding eerily familiar, but I don't say anything because I want Mo to tell me everything she knows.

"So this woman died in the park late at night. She was running by herself. Stupid, right? I mean what woman doesn't know better than to run alone at night, and in L.A. of all places?" Mo scoffs and shakes her head. "Anyway, she was found the next morning at the bottom of a ditch. Detective Acosta arrived on the crime scene and determined she fell because she couldn't see in the dark."

"Very similar to Victoria Masters's fall," Cam says.

"I thought so, too. This woman also broke her neck. Detective Acosta thought the case was closed, until about a week later, when another woman turned up dead, also with a broken neck from a supposed fall."

No way! "It was a serial killer making the deaths look like accidents?" I ask.

Mo nods. "Yup. And Detective Acosta didn't figure it out after the second death either. It took one more for him to connect the dots."

Wow. I can see why he wasn't going to just write off Victoria's death as an accident then. If he was wrong, his career would probably be over. I mean missing a clue when you're new to the job is one thing, but to have it happen again would be the end of his time in law enforcement. "Did he leave L.A. of his own volition, or was he forced out?"

"He left. The media had a field day ripping him apart and calling him incompetent. The guy had to move clear across the country to get away from that case that nearly ruined his entire career."

Now I feel bad for giving him such a hard time. I can see why he's being a jerk and really impersonal. He must be terrified to screw up again, especially because this case is similar to that one.

"I know that look, Jo," Cam says. "You feel bad for him, don't you?"

"I know he's giving me a hard time, but after hearing this, I kind of get why. Chief Harvey isn't the type to give second chances. If Detective Acosta's first case here doesn't end well, he might be moving to Fiji next."

"Does this mean you plan to help him solve the case?" Mo asks.

"Isn't that what you've been doing all along?" Cam asks.

I'm not sure if I was trying to solve the case for Detective Acosta, myself, or Quentin and Sam in a weird, messed up sort of way. I sigh. "He deserves a chance. If I can help, I will."

"And if he refuses your help?" Mo asks.

"Then I'll pretend he's Quentin, and I'll help him behind his back."

CHAPTER NINE

After we close for the day, Cam and I drive back to Columbia to talk to Thomas Masters. He's still my prime suspect, and I'm convinced he's the one who broke into Bouquets of Love and stole the restraining order.

Cam pulls up to Thomas's house and parks. This time there's a car in the driveway. It's a black BMW.

"Looks like someone has some money," Cam says.

"Or he blew it all on a nice car for appearance sake," I say.

We walk up to the front door and ring the bell. The man that answers is well groomed and wearing a suit.

"Can I help you?" he asks.

"I hope so," I say. "We'd like to speak to you about your late ex-wife."

"I have nothing to say about Vicky." He tries to close the door in our faces.

"Why did you break into her store, then?" I ask, and he reopens the door.

His eyes narrow on me. "I don't know what you're talking about. I haven't seen Vicky in months."

"I never said you saw her. I asked why you broke into her store. We know you took the copy of the restraining order."

His jaw tenses.

"Mr. Masters, we're also aware of the reason Vicky wanted a restraining order against you."

"You don't know anything. I was never in Vicky's store. I haven't gone near her in months, like I said. The last time I saw her was when we signed the divorce papers. I don't know who you people are, but I assure you if you come back here and try to harass me again, I'll call the police." He slams the door.

"He's got to be lying," Cam says. "There's no other reason for why he's being so defensive."

I'm inclined to agree. "We need to find someone who saw him in Bennett Falls. We need to prove he was there at some point."

"You want to show his picture around town?" Cam asks. "That's risky. That could definitely get back to Detective Acosta."

"I don't think we have any other choice."

When we get back home, Jamar's door is wide open. He comes out carrying Midnight. "Hey, someone's been looking for you two." He puts Midnight down on the floor, and she weaves between my legs and Cam's.

"We made a trip to New Jersey to see Thomas Masters," I say, bending down to scratch the top of Midnight's head.

"Did he actually talk to you?" Jamar asks, following us into our apartment.

"Briefly," I say. "He threatened to call the police on us if we came back."

"That sort of makes him look guilty of something, doesn't it?" Jamar leans against the kitchen counter while I get started on brewing a pot of coffee.

"I'm convinced he took the restraining order. No one else would have a reason to."

"And the only reason to take it is to keep from looking guilty," Jamar says.

"Yes, but the question is does Thomas Masters not want to look guilty so he isn't convicted of the murder he committed or is he trying to avoid being wrongfully accused?"

"You really think there's a chance he didn't do it?" Cam asks, filling Midnight's water bowl.

I shrug. "I don't know." Normally, I'd know a lot more about a case by now, but with Detective Acosta standing in my way, things are progressing a lot slower than usual.

Friday morning, all anyone can talk about is how Detective Acosta made an arrest in his case. I can't believe it myself. He arrested Thomas Masters. He had to work with the Columbia Police Department to do it, but they're allowing him to detain Masters here in Bennett Falls. Apparently, Chief Harvey is good friends with the police chief in Columbia.

"If you ask me, Jo led Acosta right to Masters," Mickey tells the table of people he's sitting with.

"I don't think the detective will appreciate you giving me the credit, Mickey," I say, refilling his coffee.

Mickey shrugs. "Who cares? We all know you've been the best detective in this town for a while now."

"I'm trying not to stay on the BFPD's bad side, though," I say.

"Okay, I'll make sure I don't say anything of the sort outside of these walls then."

"I appreciate it." I walk back to the counter. Tyler is working today. He called me last night to say he was feeling much better. He thinks it was something he ate that didn't agree with him.

"I know I'm new to town, but even I can see Mickey's not wrong about you, Jo," Tyler says. "You could run circles around any of the members of the BFPD."

Someone clears their throat, and I look up to see Detective Acosta standing at the counter. "Detective, good morning. I hear congratulations are in order."

"Thank you," he says, but his tone isn't exactly the epitome of friendly.

"You might be setting a record with how quickly you solved the case. Four days is pretty impressive." I have no idea what the record is or even if there is one, but I know Detective Acosta overheard what Tyler said, so I'm trying to smooth things over. "How about a coffee on the house to celebrate?"

"I'm not here for coffee. I need to speak to you for a moment."

"Okay." I gesture to the corner table. I'm convinced my customers leave it open for me because they're so used to me talking to Quentin—and now Detective Acosta—at that table.

He walks over to the empty table and sits down. Cam's face pops up in the kitchen window as I sit, and the next thing I know, he's at my side. "Detective," he says, placing a hand on the back of my chair to show we're a united front.

"Mr. Turner." Detective Acosta dips his head ever so slightly. "I'll get right to the point. As you know, I arrested Thomas Masters for the murder of Victoria Masters. This morning, he made a rather odd request."

"What's that?" I ask.

"He's asking to speak to you." Detective Acosta directs his gaze at me.

"Why me?"

"I wish I knew. But he told me some couple came to his house asking questions about the restraining order. I knew right away who that couple was."

I wonder if this is a case of Thomas Masters wanting to face his accusers. I find it odd that Detective Acosta is entertaining the idea. "Do you want us to talk to him?"

"I figure it can't hurt. This might mean he's willing to tell us what happened."

If Detective Acosta wants Thomas Masters to talk, it means he knows he doesn't have enough evidence against him yet. Why then did he arrest him already?

"Okay. When?" Cam asks.

"Now. The sooner the better. I want this case closed. And so do Victoria's sisters. I spoke with them before I came here."

I know Chloe is more than ready to put all of this behind her. When Robin called her yesterday to tell her how much money we made selling the flowers, she was barely interested in collecting it. And when she came by Cup of Jo to get it, she left her engine running, grabbed the envelope of cash, and left.

Tyler walks over to the table. "Can I get you all anything?" he asks.

"We're about to leave," Detective Acosta says.

"Tyler, can you and Jamar cover things here for a while. Cam and I need to go to the station with Detective Acosta. It shouldn't take long."

"No problem."

Detective Acosta stands up, and as I do the same, I see all eyes on us. Detective Acosta sighs. "Is it always like this in here?"

"Yes," I say, hoping that might convince him not to come back. I don't want him to make a habit of frequenting Cup of Jo.

"I'll follow you," he tells us, and I can't help

wondering if he doesn't trust us to go to the station otherwise.

Cam drives, making sure to observe all traffic laws. Not that Cam speeds anyway, but we're both convinced Detective Acosta would love a reason to give us a ticket.

"What do you think this is about?" Cam asks me.

"I have no idea. Maybe he wants to yell at us for getting him arrested."

"That will be fun." Cam turns into the station and parks. Detective Acosta parks right next to us.

As we walk inside, I see Officer Liberman. The way he glares at Detective Acosta tells me he's not all that fond of his new colleague. After learning about Detective Acosta's past in L.A., I would have thought he'd be careful not to ruffle feathers here. He could use some friends on the force, but it seems like he's alienating himself instead. Maybe he's afraid to make friends in case he doesn't stay here for long.

Detective Acosta brings us to an interrogation room where Thomas is waiting. Cam and I take seats across from him.

"Why did you want to speak to us?" I ask Thomas, not wasting any time at all.

"You owe it to me," he says, making me like him even less than I already did.

"How do you figure that?"

"You're the reason I'm here."

"I highly doubt that."

"No one was looking at me until you came snooping."

"You brought this on yourself." I'm not letting him intimidate me or place blame on me. He created this mess.

He scoffs. "I didn't kill Vicky."

"I have no reason to believe anything you say."

"You can't prove I touched her."

"The restraining order proves you did. I'm sure that's why you broke into Bouquets of Love and stole it."

Thomas sits forward, and for a brief moment, I think he might take a swing at me. Cam reaches a protective arm in front of me.

"If you so much as lay a fingernail on her…"

Thomas smirks. "You'll what?"

"Cam, don't. He's not worth it."

Detective Acosta looks between the three of us. "No one is laying a hand on anyone else. If you can't keep this civil, I will end this conversation right now."

"Things aren't looking good for you, Mr. Masters, so if you have anything to say that might redeem you in any way, I suggest you do it." I level him with a look.

"I don't take orders from women."

"It wasn't an order. It was a suggestion. And might I remind you that you requested our presence here. Cam and I are more than happy to leave you in Detective Acosta's hands. I personally don't care if you go to jail for murder. It doesn't affect my life in the least."

"I told you I didn't kill Vicky."

"But you did do something. You broke into her store."

"Fine. I broke into the store. You want to charge me with breaking and entering, be my guest."

"I will," Detective Acosta says before eyeing me up. I'm sure he's surprised I got Thomas Masters to confess to that much. I am, too, actually.

"You stole the restraining order," I continue. "But why? She never went through with it. It was a draft."

"I know. I talked her out of it. But I knew she kept a copy. She threatened me with it. Said if I ever came near her again, she'd follow through with filing it."

"Did you go near her again?" Detective Acosta asks.

"No." Thomas looks away, a dead giveaway that he's lying.

"You won't mind me showing your photograph around town then," I say. "Since no one would recognize you. They couldn't if you were never here, right?"

His jaw clenches, and if looks could kill, Detective Acosta would have another dead body on his hands.

"You were here. You found Vicky. Tracked her down, didn't you? Why? Were you upset she left you? That she finally stood up to you and your beatings? That she decided enough was enough?"

"Ask my girlfriend if I cared that Vicky was gone."

Girlfriend? This man clearly hates women, sees them as beneath him. Why then did he get married and have a girlfriend, possibly at the same time? "Were you having an affair?" I ask.

He looks down at his lap.

That's it. That's why Thomas Masters started hitting his wife. "Vicky found out. She confronted you, and you hit her. That's how it began. You were trying to scare her into silence. You didn't want her to divorce you, so you tried to intimidate her instead."

"I couldn't lose everything because she was jealous."

Jealous? I'm ready to lose it on this guy, but Cam beats me to it.

"You made a commitment to Vicky. She had every right to be upset when you broke your vows to her." Cam stands up and runs a hand through his hair. I know he's trying to calm down. I stand up, too, and place my hand on his arm. "She had every right to leave you and take you for all you're worth."

"That's what you were afraid of. You figured since you were unfaithful, a judge would grant her more in the divorce."

"The judge was a woman. Of course, I was going to get screwed."

He deserved it. "Why did you track down Vicky?" I ask. "Were you looking for revenge because you lost so much in the divorce?"

"I had to make sure she didn't go through with the restraining order. I wasn't going to let her ruin my reputation."

I place my hands flat on the table. "You did that all on your own, you——"

Cam grabs me by my shoulders and pulls me back.

"Easy, Jo," he whispers in my ear. "I want to hit this guy as much as you do, but we can't. Don't give Detective Acosta a reason to lock either one of us up. Masters would enjoy that too much."

"Are we finished here?" I ask Detective Acosta.

To my surprise, he dips his head.

As we head for the exit, Chief Harvey pokes his head out of his office. "Coffee, in here."

Cam laces his fingers through mine. Chief Harvey might not have invited Cam into his office, but Cam's not letting me go in there without him. We step inside.

"Chief," I say, standing behind the chairs across from him.

"Have a seat."

"We're good to stand."

He eyes me for a moment. "Suit yourself. Shut the door, though."

Cam shuts the doors. "What's this about, Chief?"

"Detective Acosta. I want to know how much help he got from you both."

"He questioned us since Cup of Jo is right next door to Bouquets of Love," I say.

"You didn't give him any tips?" One of his eyebrows rises in challenge.

"I don't know if you'd call it a tip, but we did mention that when we were inside Bouquets of Love, we found a restraining order against Thomas Masters. I'm assuming Detective Acosta felt that could implicate Mr. Masters in the break-in since the restraining order was no longer in the filing cabinet after the break-in occurred."

"You're saying Detective Acosta made that conclusion himself?" Chief Harvey asks.

"It seems that way. He arrested Thomas Masters, so I'm assuming he found other evidence."

"Let's find out. Shall we?" The chief stands up from his desk, walks to the door, and bellows Acosta's name.

Detective Acosta walks into the office, a look of confusion on his face when he sees Cam and me. "Yes, Chief?"

"Ms. Coffee and Mr. Turner tell me that the information they gave you yesterday about the restraining order was the catalyst for you arresting Mr. Masters." He's making it sound like we took the credit for it, when that's not at all what we said.

"Chief, I think you misunderstood us," I say, but he holds up a hand.

"They mentioned they saw a restraining order, one we did not find after the break-in. I deduced the only person who would steal it would be Thomas Masters since it gave him a motive for wanting to harm his ex-wife." To his credit, Detective Acosta is keeping his face devoid of emotion, even though I'm sure he's reeling on the inside.

"Very good. That's exactly what these two just told me."

Detective Acosta's expression falters for a moment as he realizes he was set up to see if our stories matched.

"Good work, Detective. You're dismissed."

Detective Acosta bows his head slightly before walking out.

"You two are also dismissed," Chief Harvey tells us.

Detective Acosta is waiting for us at the door. "I don't need you to do me any favors," Detective Acosta says.

"We didn't. We told the truth," I say. "I just hope you found enough evidence to prove Thomas's guilt. If you haven't, you might want to consider talking to his girl-friend, whoever she is."

"I don't need you to tell me how to do my job either, Ms. Coffee."

"Of course not," I say.

Despite his words, he tips his head down in the smallest nod imaginable. He's going to follow my lead yet again.

CHAPTER TEN

Mo, Wes, Cam, and I are seated at a table in Cup of Jo, eating takeout from the Chinese restaurant.

"Are you really questioning if Thomas Masters is innocent?" Mo asks, crossing her arms. "The guy beat his wife."

"Believe me I don't like him at all, but if he didn't kill her, I don't think he should go to jail for murder. I think he needs to get help for his anger issues and face the consequences of hitting his wife."

"You're much nicer than I am. I'd let him rot in jail. The guy deserves it."

"If I did that and he isn't guilty, the real killer would go free. How is that fair?" I ask. "Besides, we might end up proving he is the murderer. Who knows?"

She huffs and lowers her arms. "Fine. I guess that's true, but I still want him to suffer."

"I'm more impressed that you're helping Detective Acosta," Wes says.

"Did you see the way he acknowledged your lead at the station?" Cam asks. "It was like his mouth was saying one thing, but his head bob was saying another."

"I think he appreciated that we had his back with Chief Harvey. It earned us some brownie points."

"Plus, you gave him someone else to get information out of," Mo says. "If he can track down the girlfriend, that is."

"I'm sure Thomas Masters gave up her name. He wants the charges against him dropped, so I don't doubt he's going to tell Detective Acosta to talk to this woman. She might be his alibi."

"She could easily be lying for him, though," Mo says.

"I agree, which is why we need to find out who she is and talk to her, too."

"How do you plan to do that?" Wes asks. "If Masters was having an affair, he wouldn't publicize it."

No, he wouldn't. He's the type to be concerned with appearances. I think that's why he didn't want Victoria to divorce him. It would make him look bad. "How do we find her then?" I ask.

"You could tail Detective Acosta," Mo says with a laugh, but I'm not sure it's a bad idea.

"We could do that. He could lead us right to her."

"And we could easily get caught," Cam says. "We might finally be on Detective Acosta's good side, and you want to chance ruining it?"

"How else will we find this woman?" I ask.

"He has to know her from somewhere he works or lives," Wes says. "Maybe Mo and I can come up with a list of possibilities."

That will take too long. He could have met this woman at a bar for all we know. Or even a gas station. "No, I think we need to follow Acosta. It's the quickest way." Other than talking to Thomas Masters, which we can't do without alerting everyone at the BFPD.

"He might have already gone to see her by now," Cam says.

"Then we better not waste any more time," I say, standing up and pushing in my chair. "Can you guys clean up here?" I gesture to the food containers, which are almost empty.

"Yeah, go," Mo says. I'm surprised she didn't tell me what I'll owe for doing it. She usually makes me pay in the form of home-cooked dinners.

Cam and I let Jamar and Tyler know we might not make it back before closing. Jamar assures me he'll handle everything without any problems.

Trying to tail a police officer is more than a little complicated. We can't exactly sit in the parking lot of the police station and wait for Detective Acosta to get into his patrol car. He knows Cam's vehicle and would spot us for sure. So we park across the street from the police station in the parking lot of an apartment complex. I'm hoping we'll blend in here without being noticed.

"I wish we had binoculars," Cam says.

"We have phones. We could zoom in on the door of the police station." Anyone who saw us would probably assume we were watching videos on our phones, and having our phones in front of our faces would obstruct Detective Acosta's view of us if he does happen to have exceptional eyesight.

Officer Liberman comes out of the station and gets into his patrol car. What I don't expect is for him to come across the street to the apartment complex where we're staked out. He pulls up next to the passenger side and motions for me to lower my window.

"Officer Liberman, what are you doing here?"

"Possibly saving you two from another trip to the station. What are you up to?"

"How did you even notice us?" Cam asks, ruining my chances of lying my way out of this one.

"No offense, but you two have been to the station so much I know both of your vehicles well. I saw you drive by the station and head here. I've never seen you here before, so I figured something was up."

And he decided to check it out for himself. "You'd make a good detective, Officer Liberman."

"I'd probably wind up partners with Acosta, and I'm not sure I could handle that, so I think I'll stay where I am for now." He's also young, the youngest at the BFPD, so I doubt Chief Harvey would let him take lead on any cases for quite a while. "Tell me you two aren't working this case behind Acosta's back."

Officer Liberman is a good guy and a good cop. I

don't want to lie to him. "Thomas Masters told us to look into his girlfriend. The problem is that we don't have any idea who she is because he didn't give us her name."

Officer Liberman nods. "And you think he did give her name to Acosta."

"You're right again."

"How do you plan to stalk him without him noticing? It's sort of in his job description to be highly aware of his surroundings. I think he'd notice you tailing him and showing up everywhere he went."

"We just need to know where to look for the girl-friend. If Thomas Masters wants us to talk to her, then I want to know why."

"Want me to get you in there to see him?"

I can't believe he'd offer to do that. "How? Isn't Detective Acosta in there?"

"Nope. He's most likely questioning the mystery girl-friend as we speak. I could get you in there to see Thomas Masters, but I can't stop him from telling Acosta he talked to you."

That would get Officer Liberman in trouble because it would get back to Detective Acosta that Liberman was the one who let Cam and me in. I can't ask him to do that. "We appreciate the offer, but I don't want you getting into trouble for us."

"Okay, I have another offer then. I'll go talk to Masters and see if he'll give me the name."

"Aren't you afraid he'll tell Acosta you were asking questions?" Cam asks.

Officer Liberman bobs one shoulder. "Masters was running his mouth before. The guy likes to hear himself talk. I could tell Acosta that Masters was running his mouth again and insisting we confirm his alibi with his girlfriend. It makes sense he'd let her name slip."

That might work, but I still hate to put Officer Liberman in the middle of this. "Are you sure about this?"

"Tell you what. You wait here. If I don't come back in fifteen minutes, I decided not to go through with it. Go home and call it a day."

"Fair enough," I say.

He nods and starts to back out.

"Officer Liberman," I call to him.

He stops the car.

"Thanks for being a bright spot at the BFPD."

He smiles and pulls out of the lot.

"Think he'll get the name?" Cam asks.

I think Officer Liberman has a lot of potential. He's likeable, too. "I have no doubt he'll get the information we need. I just hope he doesn't get caught by Detective Acosta or Chief Harvey."

"Same here."

We sit and wait. Cam really is scrolling through videos on his phone now. They appear to be baking videos. I'm still watching the door of the police station. After thirteen minutes pass, I'm about to give up hope. I can't blame Officer Liberman if he decides not to risk his career for this. He doesn't owe us anything, and I really don't want to get him in trouble with the chief. But then I see him come out of the station again.

"How do you think he explained leaving and returning so soon the first time?" Cam asks.

I didn't think of that, but he was only gone for the few minutes he spoke to us. It might look suspicious to a group of cops. "Maybe he said he needed gas or something like that." There is a gas station on the road.

"He's coming this way," Cam says.

Once again, Officer Liberman pulls up beside me. My window is still lowered, so I say, "How did it go?"

"Well for you two, but not well for Delila Sommers. That's the girlfriend's name. And get this. She lives here in Bennett Falls."

No way! No wonder Thomas Masters was able to find Victoria after she moved here. Victoria moved to the same town his mistress lives in. What are the odds of that? I don't think she could have known because there's no way she'd willingly move closer to the woman who started the decline of her marriage.

"This is great. If she lives in town, we'll have no trouble finding her. Thank you, Officer Liberman. Please come into Cup of Jo soon. We owe you free coffee and pastries."

"I'll happily take you up on that offer, but this conversation never happened. You're simply offering free stuff to me because I'm an officer of the law and work hard to keep this town safe."

"Isn't that what I said?" I smile at him.

He returns the smile before driving away.

"Let's go," I say.

"Where? I didn't even see you look up an address for Delila Sommers."

"I didn't. Detective Acosta is there now, remember? We'll go see her tonight. Right now, I want to talk to Chloe and Hazel Francis. We need to find out if they knew about the affair."

Cam drives us to Chloe Francis's house, but she's not home.

"She's meeting with a client," Hazel says, letting us into the living room. Chloe has a lot of lunch and dinner meetings since she works from home. I'm not sure how she can go on with life as usual like this." She looks around. "Would you two like coffee or something?"

"No, thank you. We're fine. We just wanted to ask you a question."

"Sure."

"Do you know anyone named Delila Sommers?"

Hazel pauses as if trying to place the name. "No, sorry. Who is she?"

"According to Thomas Masters, she's his girlfriend and was his mistress when he was still married to Vicky."

"What?" Hazel practically shrieks. "He was cheating on Vicky?"

"She never told you?" Cam asks.

"No. When they started fighting, I asked her what happened, and she said he'd changed." She scoffs. "I can't believe this. Why wouldn't she tell me the truth?"

"I don't know," I say. "Maybe she was embarrassed."

"She had nothing to be embarrassed about. He's the lowlife cheater."

"I agree. I hate cheaters, but I think Vicky was embarrassed that the man she chose to spend the rest of her life with wound up cheating on her and ruining their marriage."

Hazel inhales sharply. "Is that why he hit her? Did she try to stand up for herself?"

I nod. "We think so, yes."

Hazel breaks down and cries. She slumps into the armchair in the process. "How didn't I know any of this. For the longest time, Vicky told us she started taking kickboxing, and that's where the bruises came from. When she finally divorced him, she said he hurt her. I thought maybe she was making it up because I'd never seen Thomas act cruelly to her. I thought she was angry that her marriage was over and that's why she was trying to make him out to be a monster. I even told her to drop the restraining order because it was going too far and she was going to destroy his reputation. I had no idea he'd really done those things to her." She's full-on sobbing now.

The front door opens, and Chloe walks in. "Hazel?" she calls, but she doesn't have to ask where Hazel is. The loud sobbing leads Chloe right to us. "What's going on? Is she okay?" She rushes over to put her arm around her sister.

"We discovered Thomas Masters was having an affair

while he was married to your sister," Cam says in a soft voice.

"I didn't believe her," Hazel says, latching onto Chloe's arms. "I feel awful. I should have listened to her."

"It's not your fault. You didn't know. Why is the affair important anyway?" Chloe asks, looking at Cam and me.

"Thomas Masters told us about it. I think he's trying to use this woman as his alibi for the night Vicky died."

Hazel stands up and wipes her cheeks. "He needs to pay for what he did to Vicky. I'm not going to sit back and watch him get away with this, especially with his mistress helping him do it. There's no justice in that. This is all his fault." She's switched gears rather quickly.

"I'm sure the police will sort it all out, Hazel. Try to calm down." Chloe is the picture of calm. Her emotions have been so erratic since we've met her.

"We came by to see if either of you knew Delila Sommers," I say.

Chloe inhales sharply. "Did you say Delila Sommers?"

She knows her. Worse, the horror on her face tells me how she knows her. "She's one of your clients, isn't she?"

Chloe sits down in the chair Hazel vacated. "Yes. I met her about a year ago. She had just moved into town from—"

"Columbia, New Jersey," I say.

She bobs her head. "We bonded over the fact that she lived where my sister and her new husband had been living for the past ten months." She shakes her head. "Do you know how long Thomas and Delila have been seeing each other?"

"Not really, but I'm willing to bet it was during the first ten months of his marriage to your sister." The honeymoon period hadn't even passed, and Thomas had found himself another woman on the side. What a sleaze.

"I can't believe I helped her. I designed her entire home. The home she was using to sneak around with my brother-in-law." She puts her head in her hands. "This is too much."

"I'm so sorry." How do I ask her for Delila's address now? I can't do it. I'll get Mo to look it up if need be. "We should go. I'm sorry we've bothered you."

"No." Chloe raises her head. "Will you do me a favor?"

I owe her one after the grief we've caused both her and Hazel today. "Of course."

"Will you go see Delila and find out when she started seeing Thomas? And if she was with him Sunday night into Monday morning?" She wants to know if Thomas was in Bennett Falls that night and could have killed Vicky.

"If you have an address, we'll go there now," I say.

She pulls her phone from her back pocket and scrolls through her contacts. "What's your number? I'll text you the address."

I rattle off my number, and a few seconds later, my phone dings with her message.

"It's probably stupid, but I want to know what she says. I have to know. I'll go crazy here thinking of possible scenarios, and I don't know what I'll do."

Is she saying she'll go after Delila and Thomas herself? I look at Hazel. Poor Hazel, who is barely keeping it together. She can't handle having one sister dead and the other locked up for attempted murder or assault.

CHAPTER ELEVEN

"That was intense," Cam says.

"Very. I'm scared of what Chloe might do to Delila. I mean Delila must have known Chloe was Vicky's sister. As soon as they started talking about Vicky and Thomas, Delila would have had a clear picture of what was going on, even if she had no idea Thomas was married before that." Although, I'm pretty sure Delila did know she was messing around with a married man. How could she not? There are too many signs to miss. The wedding band, or tan from one if he took it off. Needing to be home every evening. Phone calls from the same woman all the time. My opinion of Delila isn't very good at all, and I haven't even laid eyes on her yet.

"This is interesting," Cam says as he pulls up to a huge house on what looks like a horse farm. "If Delila lives here, she's got money. So why would someone so obsessed with appearances like Thomas Masters stay with Vicky instead of marrying Delila?"

He makes a good point. Delila looks very well off. We park in the driveway and walk up to the house, which has a massive double door. Cam rings the bell.

The woman who answers is wearing riding gear. "Can I help you?"

"Hi, are you Delila Sommers?" I ask.

"Yes. Why are you asking? If you don't know who I am, you most certainly have no business being here."

"Thomas Masters sent us," I say, hoping that will take her down a notch.

She steps outside and closes the door behind her. "I don't know anyone by that name."

Oh, now things are starting to make sense. "Thomas wasn't the only one having an affair. You're married."

"Excuse me, but I have no idea who you are, so I can assure you that you don't know anything about me."

"I know you moved here from Columbia, New Jersey, where you met Thomas Masters, a married man, but I guess that didn't matter since you yourself were married. Let me guess, this is your husband's money you're living off of. That's why you and Thomas were sneaking around. You married for money, not love, and he married someone who would make him look good. Neither one of you cared about your spouses."

Her mouth hangs open for a moment. "You need to get off my property this instant."

"I'm not finished yet. You moved here to Bennett

Falls about a year ago, and you hired an interior designer by the name of Chloe Francis. You didn't realize at the time that she was Thomas's sister-in-law, but you figured it out pretty quickly once she started asking you questions about where you were from."

"How did you keep a straight face when she told you all about her sister and brother-in-law?" Cam asks.

"I was in shock. That's the honest truth." Delila starts walking toward the barn on the side of the house, and we follow. "I knew Thomas was married. He told me as much. But he said he married her because his family approved of her, and they were difficult to please. His money comes from his grandmother, and she would only give him his trust fund if he married a woman she approved of. That was Victoria."

And Victoria had no idea she was nothing more than a means to an end.

She walks over to the black horse in the first stall and strokes its head. "I was newly married when I met Thomas. My family had no money. As a kid, I got my clothing from thrift stores and those donation bins you see in parking lots. You have no idea what it was like growing up like that. So when I met my husband, Liam, I did what I had to do to help my family."

"You married him to get to his money," Cam says.

"He's a good man. Kind. But I didn't love him. I think he knew it, too. He was always buying me things. Sending my parents on vacations. I think he thought he could buy my love, but as much as I tried to love him, I just couldn't." She grabs a sugar cube from her pocket and feeds it to the horse.

"But you and Thomas, you love each other?" Cam asks.

"I know what you're thinking. He's older than I am. Yes, he is. But that doesn't matter to me. I mean look around. If I cared about superficial things, I'd be madly in love with my husband. I did this for my family. I couldn't let them wind up living on the street." She wipes a tear that falls from her left eye. "But when I met Thomas at the bar one night, we just clicked. There was this spark I'd never felt with anyone else. I knew what I was doing was wrong, but I figured if Liam and Victoria never found out, we wouldn't be hurting them."

I know I'll never be able to explain to her why that's absurd. "Did you know Victoria moved to Bennett Falls?"

She nods. "I wasn't happy about it."

"Why not?" Why would she care? It's not like Victoria and Thomas were still married.

"You know what it's like with exes. Do you ever really get over them?"

"Yes," I say. "That's why they're your ex and not your significant other."

She cocks her head at me. "You can't have many exes then."

Not many, no. Quentin and I were together for a while. Before him, I didn't have a lot of relationships. I was more interested in hanging out with my friends in high school. And Quentin and Cam were both included in that group. They've been my two biggest relationships in my life. I don't want to discuss this with Delila, though.

"Did you think Thomas still had feelings for Victoria?" Cam asks.

"I thought you said he only married her to get his grandmother's money."

"He did, and when they got divorced, some of his cousins tried to petition his grandmother's will, claiming Thomas should have to give the money back." Delila feeds the horse another sugar cube.

"You were afraid he'd come here and try to talk Victoria into getting back together with him," I say.

She bobs one shoulder. "I know he loves me, but I don't want him to be married to her again. It's much easier for us to see each other when he's single."

Two possible scenarios are running through my mind. In the first, Thomas went to see Victoria at the flower shop to talk her into getting back together, but she refused. Thomas got angry and shoved her down the stairs. In the second scenario, Delila went to confront Victoria at the flower shop and they fought over Thomas, resulting in Delila pushing Victoria down the stairs.

Either way, I think the affair is most likely the root of all the trouble.

"Did you talk to Victoria?" Cam asks.

Delila turns away from us and focuses on the horse. I have to wonder if she doesn't want to look at us because lying to someone's face is ten times more difficult than just saying the lie to open space, or a nonjudgmental animal like a horse. "I was there over the weekend when she was moving things in. I pretended to be stopping in to inquire about the types of arrangements she was going to be selling."

I was under the impression Victoria knew who Delila was. "She didn't recognize you?" I ask.

"Not at first. I was wearing sunglasses and a big sun hat. We were outside."

Then people must have seen them together. Witnesses could probably place Delila with Victoria.

"When did she realize who you were?" I ask.

Delila turns back toward us. "It was my perfume. It's called Fiji sunrise. She recognized the scent. I guess Thomas came home smelling like it on more than one occasion."

"Did she seem upset?" Cam asks.

Delila bobs her shoulder. "Not really. She asked about the perfume, and then she asked if I knew Thomas. I debated denying it, but I decided since they were divorced, there was no point."

Not to mention she didn't want Victoria and Thomas getting back together. She wanted to make it clear to Victoria that Thomas was still with her.

"How did she react?" Cam asks.

"She threatened me."

I wasn't expecting that. Victoria seemed like the type of woman who had trouble standing up for herself. It took her a while to divorce Thomas, and he was physically abusing her. She didn't follow through with the restraining order either. Confronting Delila and threatening her doesn't fit with Victoria's character at all.

"How so?" Cam asks.

"She told me I better be careful or I was going to end up with bruises all over me or worse."

It wasn't a threat at all. "Delila, Victoria was trying to warn you. Thomas used to beat her."

Delila shakes her head. "No way. Thomas wouldn't hurt anyone."

She clearly doesn't know the Thomas we know. "You've never seen that side of him?" I ask. "Even Victoria and Thomas's neighbors in Columbia knew he was beating her. They saw Victoria's bruises."

"She was lying then. Trying to ruin his reputation. He'd never do something like that. It's completely absurd. I'm not going to let you run his name through the mud like this."

"Is that what you told Victoria?" I ask. "Did you threaten her?"

Delila takes a step back, but the stall behind her stops her. "What are you really asking?"

"Jo, easy," Cam says.

"I'm asking if you fought with Victoria and pushed her down the stairs to save your boyfriend's reputation?"

Delila throws her arm out, pointing toward the driveway. "Get off my property this instant! I'm calling the police."

"That won't be necessary," Cam says. "We're leaving." He takes my hand and walks me back to the car. "Why did you come out and accuse her like that?"

"I wanted to see her reaction. She easily could have done this, Cam."

"I agree, but we have no authority to arrest her or even detain her. And we have no police backup anymore." He opens the passenger door for me and looks back at the stable. "She's on her phone."

Great. We can expect a visit from Detective Acosta very soon. This day is about to get a whole lot worse.

When we get back to Cup of Jo, there's a patrol car waiting for us out front. Cam and I exchange a look before we get out of the SUV. We can't dodge the police, so there's no point in trying. Cup of Jo is closed for the day, so I'm not sure why Detective Acosta thought to wait for us here instead of going to our apartment. Once Detective Acosta sees us, he gets out of his patrol car and stands in front of the SUV.

"Detective," I say as soon as I get out of the car.

"I thought I'd made myself clear," he says.

"About?" Playing dumb is probably not my best idea, but I'll admit I'm a little nervous at the moment.

"Tell me why Delila Sommers called to say two people came on to her property and were harassing her."

"We didn't harass her. She willingly talked to us."

Cam joins me on the passenger side of the car. "When she asked us to leave, we did so without pause."

"Why were you there to begin with?"

"Thomas Masters told us to talk to his girlfriend. You

126

heard him. You were right there with us in that interrogation room, so if anything—"

"Jo," Cam says in a low voice. He knows very well I was about to tell Detective Acosta it was his fault we spoke to Thomas Masters in the first place.

"What were you going to say, Ms. Coffee?" Detective Acosta asks, placing his hands on his hips.

"She was going to say if anything we said upset Mrs. Sommers, she only has Thomas Masters to blame for sending us there." Cam's recovery is brilliant. He's equally equipped in brains and beauty.

"I see. I guess I missed the part where you two became police detectives because I don't recall Thomas Masters telling you the name of his girlfriend."

"Really?" I ask, looking at Cam. "I'm sure he mentioned it. How else would we know it?"

"I'll have to review the tape of the interrogation," Detective Acosta says with a smug smile.

If he does, he'll confirm we're lying. "If you'd like to waste your time, go right ahead, but you might want to question Delila Sommers instead."

"Why is that?" he asks, crossing his arms.

"She admitted she went to see Victoria over the weekend. From what she said, things got a little heated between them."

This is clearly news to him. "She told you that?"

"She said Victoria threatened her, but we realized that's not really what Victoria was doing. She was trying to warn Delila that Thomas has a history of hitting women. Delila misinterpreted Victoria's words, thinking Victoria was threatening to hit her."

"Did they fight?"

"That's what we were asking about when she kicked us off her property."

Detective Acosta lets out a loud puff of air. "You two need to stay away from this. I'll handle it."

"Are you going to talk to Delila?" I ask.

He starts for his patrol car. "What I do isn't your concern, Ms. Coffee. Why don't we both agree to do our jobs. I'll solve this case, and you can go back to making coffee. Stick to what you're good at."

A bigger person might be able to let his thinly veiled insult slide, but I'm five foot six. Both my height and my patience are average. "I'm good at a lot of things, Detective. For instance, I'm really good a solving cases before the police."

He pauses with his hand on the door handle. "How good are you at evading charges for interfering with an open investigation?"

Considering I'm not in jail for all the cases I interfered with when Quentin was part of the BFPD, I'd say pretty darn good. "I'm here, aren't I?"

"We'll see for how long." He gets in his car and pulls away in a hurry.

CHAPTER TWELVE

I barely sleep all night, and Saturday morning, I have big, dark circles under my eyes. I do my best to conceal them, but the look Mo gives me when she and Wes walk into Cup of Jo tells me I wasn't successful.

"What happened to you?" Mo asks.

"I had it out with the new detective. He's looking for any reason to arrest me at this point."

"Good job, Jo. I always thought it was your history with Quentin that made him threatened to handcuff you so often, but I'm starting to think you have a problem with law enforcement in general."

"That's really helpful. Thanks, baby sister."

"You know I hate when you call me that," she says.

"Yup." I turn around to grab the double shot of espresso I just made and take a sip.

"I'd love one. Thanks," Mo says.

I roll my eyes and brew another. "What can I get for you, Wes?" I ask.

"I'm not picky. Whatever is easiest for you is fine. You seem like you're having a rough morning."

"It's so nice of you to consider my well-being." I smile at him and then glare at Mo.

"Why do I feel like you like him better than you like me?" she asks.

"Because right now I do." I hand her the espresso and then make Wes a mocha. Is it the easiest drink to make? Not at all, but I know it's going to bug Mo that I made him a drink she loves when all she got was an espresso. She should know better than to mess with me before I'm sufficiently caffeinated.

"I have something that might cheer you up a bit," Wes says. "I found out that Victoria Masters wasn't the only one who tried to rent Bouquets of Love."

"Really?" I hand him his mocha.

"Hey!" Mo protests. "What gives?"

"I like him better. I thought we'd already established that." I grab a chocolate stick and place it in Wes's cup. He smiles at me, but it quickly fades when Mo shoots him a look. "Don't even think about threatening to break up with him if he drinks that," I tell her. "I will call Mom on you." Mom loves Wes. He's the only guy who can control Mo's temper. And as tough as Mo can be, Mom can be tougher.

Mo pouts and sips her espresso.

"Thank you," Wes mouths to me.

I give him a discreet nod in response. "So who else tried to rent the space next door?" I ask.

"This guy named Phillip Witte. Apparently, he had talked to Mr. DiAngelo about renting, and then Victoria swooped in and stole the place from him."

"How?" I ask.

"That I don't know. You might need to ask Mr. DiAngelo, but I'm mentioning it because Phillip Witte has a record."

If Mr. DiAngelo found that out, I understand why he decided not to rent to Phillip, especially if Vicky came along at that time ready to rent the space.

"What for?" Mo asks.

"Theft, breaking and entering, and possession of stolen goods."

"Sounds like Mr. D dodged a bullet there," Mo says.

"Breaking and entering?" I bite my bottom lip. "I wonder if the break-in next door wasn't about the restraining order at all. Maybe it was Phillip trying to get revenge on Victoria and Mr. DiAngelo."

"But Victoria was already dead. Anyone in town would have seen that on the news."

I'm not one to watch the news very often, and I doubt I'm the only one in town like that.

"What about the missing restraining order? Do you think Thomas just happened to stumble across the flower shop when the door was wide open from the break-in and helped himself?" She finishes the espresso. "Mocha, please," she says with a sweet smile.

I take her empty espresso cup. "Address and phone number for this Phillip Witte, please," I counter.

"Fine." She takes out her phone and starts searching as I make the mocha.

"Hey, you two," Cam says, coming out of the kitchen. "Are you working today?"

"Only for a few hours," Wes says.

"Wes found another possible suspect for the break-in," I tell Cam.

"Really? That's certainly interesting. I was convinced this all had to do with Thomas and Delila."

I was, too, but I don't like to leave any stone unturned. The fact that Phillip Witte wanted to rent the store and has a history of breaking and entering is too much to ignore. He had motive and prior experience.

"Are you going to tip off Detective Acosta?" Cam asks.

"I'm not sure how I can without telling him we're still investigating."

"What about an anonymous call to the station?" Mo suggests. "You see that all the time on television shows."

"Can't they trace the call, though?" I ask.

"If the call is made from a public place that doesn't have video surveillance, you'll be fine."

"Such as where?" I ask.

"I don't know. You can't expect me to think of everything."

I hand her the mocha, but I don't release my grip on it yet. "Address and phone number?"

"I'm sending it to you now."

My phone vibrates in my back pocket, and I release the drink.

"You married into a strange family, man," Wes says to Cam.

"You get used to them," he says with a smile. "And you're still here, so I think you and I are in the same boat."

Wes bobs his head.

Customers start to come in for the day, so Mo and Wes say goodbye and head across the street.

"You want to check out this guy Wes found?" Cam asks.

"I do. Even if he only broke into the store, it's still helpful in piecing together what happened to Victoria."

"Okay, well, I'm almost finished with the morning supply of baked goods. I'll be right back." He squeezes my elbow before disappearing inside the kitchen.

Tyler comes up to the counter, a dish towel slung over his shoulder. "All the tables are freshly cleaned," he says.

"Thanks, Tyler. Robin should be here any minute."

"You're leaving, aren't you?" he asks.

"For a little bit, yes."

He leans closer to me and whispers, "Then I think I should tell you that there's a patrol car parked outside."

Detective Acosta is watching us. Unbelievable! How

does he think this is a better use of his time than solving the case?

"Thanks for the heads-up, Tyler. Cam and I will have to leave out the back. Will you do me a favor and let me know if Detective Acosta comes in while we're gone?"

"Sure. No problem. What should I tell him if he asks for you?"

So many things run through my mind, but every single one would get Tyler placed in handcuffs for saying them aloud to a police detective. "If he comes inside, tell him Cam and I went out on a supply run and will be back soon. Then call me so we can get back here immediately."

"Got it."

The second Robin arrives, I go into the kitchen to tell Cam the change in plans. "We're being watched," I say. "We need to leave out the back door."

"How do you know Detective Acosta doesn't have another officer out back?" Cam asks.

"I don't. It's a chance we're going to have to take."

Cam finishes placing the muffins on the cooling rack, and then he slowly opens the back door.

"Don't look suspicious. If anyone's out there, we're going on a supply run. It can't look like we're searching the lot for a patrol car."

"Good point." He pushes open the door and plasters a fake smile on his face. "How's this?"

"Good. And to anyone observing us, it looks like we're having a normal conversation."

"One problem. My car is around the front."

I forgot about that. I dial Mo. "Where's your car parked?" I ask as soon as she picks up.

"Why?"

"We need to borrow it. Detective Acosta is out front watching Cup of Jo."

I hear movement on the other end of the line. "Yes, he is," Mo says. "My car is parked behind my office building. I'll meet you back there with the keys."

"Thanks, Mo." As much as we can push each other's buttons, we always come through for each other in times of need. I could tell her I need to bury a body, and she'd help me without asking questions until it was taken care of. Okay, maybe she wouldn't go that far. Unless the body was Quentin's. She'd be all in if that were the case. Of course, she might also be the reason we had his body on our hands in the first place. She called dibs on killing him the second she found out he cheated on me.

Cam and I jog through the joint parking lot shared by the bank and post office behind Main Street. When we come out, we're on the opposite side of the road, hopefully too far for Detective Acosta to notice us as we cross Main Street and cut around Second Street to the lot behind Mo's office building.

Mo is standing outside of her car when we get there, her keys in hand. "I'll keep an eye on him from my office window," she says.

"Thank you. I'm hoping he gets bored and leaves

soon. He should be doing his job." After all, that's what he suggested we both do, our jobs.

"Good luck." Mo hands me the keys, and I get into the driver's seat. Phillip Witte lives in the not so nice section of town. I'm guessing he's out of work since his plan to rent Bouquets of Love fell through, and that should hopefully mean we'll find him at home.

I pull up to the small ranch and cut the engine. There's a car in the driveway, so we might be in luck.

As we approach the front door, a dog starts barking inside the house. It sounds like a pretty big dog, too. We don't even get a chance to knock before a man opens the door, a Doberman pincher at his side.

"Who are you?"

"Hi," Cam says. "I'm Cam, and this is Jo. We own Cup of Jo and heard you were interested in renting the space next door."

"I was, but some woman got the space instead."

Is it possible he doesn't know Victoria is dead? "You haven't heard?" I ask.

"Heard what?"

The dog gives one sharp bark.

"The woman who was renting the space was found dead Monday morning."

The man cocks his head. "Did she die in the flower shop?"

"I'm afraid so. She broke her neck falling down the stairs."

"Really? That's some bad luck."

"I guess you're like me and don't watch much news," I say.

"Don't own a TV." He narrows his eyes at us. "Why are you here?"

"Oh, well, um, we heard you were interested in renting the space and thought we'd make sure you knew it was available again."

"How'd you find out I was interested? Did that landlord tell you?"

"Mr. DiAngelo? No. Cup of Jo is sort of a hot spot for town gossip. One of our customers mentioned it to us."

"Well, I'm not interested in renting any place where someone died. I don't need ghosts haunting my place of business."

"Oh, okay. Have you been inside the space, though? It's really nice. You might want to consider checking it out."

"I've been in there. I went after that woman got the space."

"Oh, so you met Victoria?" I ask.

"Yeah. I wanted to see why I lost out on the place when I was convinced I was getting it."

I'm guessing it was the background check Mr. DiAngelo ran on Phillip, but Phillip seems to be sure Victoria was to blame.

"She was pretty. I bet she charmed her way into the space. Women are like that. They'll put on a nice outfit, makeup, and such, and then they'll bat their eyelashes to get what they want."

"Mr. DiAngelo isn't like that," I say, trying not to let on that I'm highly insulted by his comment about women.

Phillip scoffs. "He's a man. He's like that."

Okay, so it's not just women that Phillip doesn't like. Apparently, it's the human race in general.

"What happened when you went to see Victoria?" Cam asks.

"Nothing. I asked her what she did to get the place over me. She got all offended and told me to leave her alone."

"And you left?" I ask.

He doesn't answer.

"What day was that?" Cam asks.

"Sunday."

I still don't know if Victoria died Sunday night or Monday morning. Detective Acosta hasn't shared that information with me. "You spoke to her inside the flower shop, right? Was anyone else there?"

"No. Why? What's with all the questions?"

"The police are trying to figure out who was the last one to see her on Sunday," I say. "We thought maybe you saw someone or left because someone else came into the shop."

"No. She got upset, but I wasn't having it. I'm the one who got screwed over here. She stole my rental property. It was my ticket out of this dump." He holds out his hands, and the dog barks again, as if emphasizing his owner's comment.

"What did you do?" I ask.

"I told her she'd get what was coming to her."

For the first time, I wish Detective Acosta was here because I'm pretty sure Phillip Witte just implicated himself for murder.

CHAPTER THIRTEEN

Cam wraps an arm around me. "Well, I think we've taken up enough of your time, Mr. Witte. You should stop into Cup of Jo. We'll be happy to treat you with some coffee and pastries on the house." He spins me around and directs me toward the car.

"He gives me the creeps," I say.

"Same. And he admitted to arguing with Victoria the night she died."

"We don't know she died Sunday night."

"No one saw her after that, right?"

"We should ask Chloe and Hazel," I say.

Instead of going back to Cup of Jo, we head to Chloe Francis's house. She's home when we knock on the door.

"What brings you two by?" she asks us.

"We were just wondering if you saw Victoria Sunday night," I say.

She shakes her head. "I got home late. I was out with

clients. I take them for drinks sometimes. Hazel was home, but she goes to bed pretty early. Victoria was setting things up in the store Sunday evening. I'm not sure what time she got back or if she did at all. The hours she was keeping trying to get the flower shop ready were pretty crazy."

"Is Hazel around?" I ask, trying to see past her into the house.

"Yeah, she's in her room. I know she's eager to go home. She wants nothing to do with Bennett Falls anymore, but the funeral is this evening, so she's sticking around until after that."

"We understand," Cam says.

"Come on in. I'll get her for you." She steps aside to let us inside the house and then closes the door behind us.

Cam and I wait in the entryway. We don't plan to stay long. We just need to get a timeline of events.

Hazel comes out of her room, hugging her midsection. "Hi."

"Hi, Hazel. We're sorry to bother you, but we were curious if you saw Victoria Sunday night?"

"What do you mean?" she asks.

"We're trying to figure out if she came home that evening," Cam says.

"I was in bed."

"So you don't know if she came home?" I ask.

"I didn't see her. I'm always in bed by nine thirty. I'm not a night person."

Then Victoria could have come home after Hazel fell asleep. "Did you see her in the morning?" If Hazel's not a night person, it could mean she's a morning person and was awake before her sisters. If so, she'd know if Victoria was here in the morning.

"No."

That means Victoria was most likely killed Sunday night and never came back to the house. "Thank you, Hazel. We're sorry to have bothered you."

She nods and swallows so hard I see it.

"I'll walk you out," Chloe says.

"What time are the services tonight?" Cam asks. "We'd like to go and pay our respects."

"Five to seven. It's at the funeral home on Silver Lake Road."

Cam nods. "We'll see you there."

My phone rings as we get back into the car. "It's Mo," I tell Cam before I answer it.

"Jo, you guys better get back here. Detective Acosta just went inside Cup of Jo."

"Thanks, Mo."

I know Tyler will be calling us as soon as he gets the chance. "We need supplies," I tell Cam. "And an alibi."

"I can go to the food store. If we get a receipt, it will confirm where we were."

"Smart thinking. Hurry."

We race to the food store, and Cam heads directly to the baking aisle while I go get on line. We need to expedite this process as much as possible. The person in front of me just finishes paying when Cam joins me in line, his arms full of bags of flour and sugar. He puts it all on the conveyor belt. "That was a workout," he tells me.

The girl at the register smiles at him. "You're strong," she says.

I'm tempted to tell her he's also married, but we don't have time for delays, so I let it slide. Cam pays with his credit card, and I grab the receipt with my left hand so the cashier can see my wedding ring.

"Subtle," Cam says as we bring the bags to the car. "I saw what you did there. You know you don't ever have to worry about me being unfaithful."

"I know," I say as we quickly get back on the road. "I just don't like when women openly flirt with married men."

"Neither do I," he says.

Luckily the food store is close to Cup of Jo. We park Mo's car around back and bring the bags into the kitchen. I can hear Detective Acosta's voice through the window into the dining area.

"Stay here. I'll go take care of him," I say. I push through the door. "Tyler, thanks for holding down the fort. I think we bought every bag of sugar and flour they had." I put my purse under the counter and tie on my apron. "Oh, Detective, sorry I didn't see you there."

"Where were you?"

"In the kitchen helping Cam carry in all the supplies we had to run out and buy. One of our usual deliveries was delayed, so we had to go to the food store and pay nearly twice as much." I shake my head and huff, feigning frustration. "What can you do, though, right? We can't exactly tell our customers we're out of baked goods."

"You've been gone for a while," he says.

"The place was packed. You know what weekends in a food store are like."

"It's funny. Your vehicle is still parked out front."

"Yeah, my sister had to work this morning, and her car was making a funny noise. Cam offered to take it for a spin to see if he could identify the problem." Cam doesn't know much about cars. He could whip up any dessert blindfolded, but I don't think he's ever changed the oil in a car before. I'm not sure I'm pulling off this lie well at all. My acting skills have improved, but they're still not the greatest.

"Oh, she mentioned that when she was here yesterday," Tyler says, coming to my rescue. "It sounded to me like it was a problem with the timing belt. It can cause a squeaking or rubbing sound when it needs to be changed."

I have no idea what he's talking about, but Detective Acosta seems to be buying it. "I'll tell her. She should really take it in to a mechanic."

"Definitely," Tyler says.

"So you were at the food store?" Detective Acosta asks.

"Yeah, would you like to see my receipt?" Before he can answer, I pull the receipt from my pocket, where I left it for this exact reason. "There you go. Time stamped and everything."

He looks it over. "That is a rip off for flour."

"That's what I was saying."

He hands the receipt back to me.

"How's the case coming along? Were you able to figure out if Thomas and Delila conspired together to get rid of Victoria?"

"I'm afraid I can't discuss that with you."

"Right." I bob my head. "Well, I assume you're here for some coffee before you get back to work. What can I get for you?"

He looks around, making it clear he never intended to order anything.

I hold up a finger before turning around to pour a large dark roast for him. "Here. On the house."

"Thank you." He takes the drink and places it on the counter in front of him. Then he removes his wallet from his pocket and places a five-dollar bill into the tip jar next to the register.

"That's really not necessary, Detective."

"I think it is. I don't like to owe anyone any favors." He returns the wallet to his pocket and picks up his drink. "Good day, Ms. Coffee." He turns and walks out.

"Thanks for your help with the car thing, Tyler," I say.

"No problem. I don't really care for that guy."

"Neither do I."

"I'll go fill in Cam about the car conversation."

"Thanks. I don't know what I would have come up with if he'd asked me," Cam says.

"I should tell Mo as well in case Detective Acosta asks her about it." I quickly call her, not wanting there to be any evidence in the form of text messages that the conversation took place.

"Got it," she says. "I'm due for an oil change, so I'll even call the mechanic and take the car in today."

"You're the best," I say before ending the call.

I think I have all the bases covered now, so I duck into the back office and call Mr. DiAngelo.

"Hello?" he answers.

"Hi, Mr. DiAngelo. It's Joanna Coffee."

"Oh, hello, Jo. To what do I owe the pleasure of this call? You and Cam aren't thinking of renovating again, are you?"

When Cam and I joined forces to run Cup of Jo together, we had to get Mr. DiAngelo on board with knocking down the wall between Cup of Jo and Cam's Kitchen. Luckily, the space originally used to be one rental and not two, so Mr. D. was okay with us doing it. We got really fortunate there. "No, no renovations this time. We're very happy with the space."

"Good, then what can I do for you?" he asks.

"I was curious about the man who wanted to rent Bouquets of Love, Phillip Witte. I was wondering if you wouldn't mind telling me why you decided not to rent to him."

Mr. DiAngelo sighs. "You know I run background

checks on everyone I rent to. I have to be careful with my properties. They're my sole source of income."

"Of course."

"Well, Mr. Witte doesn't have the cleanest record. I decided it wasn't in my best interest to rent to him. Ms. Masters came along at the same time, so I took it as a sign. Although, looking back on it now, I'm not sure I fared much better in the end."

No, he didn't. Trying to rent a property where a murder occurred won't be easy.

"I'm crossing my fingers the police rule this an accidental death. If not, I might be trying to encourage you and Cam to expand Cup of Jo further." He gives a small laugh, but I can hear the concern in his voice. He depends on that income. "I'm sorry. I probably sound really callous right now. A woman died, and I'm worried about money."

"You have to pay the bills just like the rest of us. I know you don't mean any disrespect to Victoria Masters."

"Well, if you hear of anyone who's looking to rent, please send them my way. I'm almost tempted to see if Phillip Witte is still interested."

I don't bother telling him Phillip is afraid of ghosts. I don't think Mr. DiAngelo will really reach out to Phillip anyway. "I will, Mr. D. Talk to you soon." I end the call.

I'm not convinced Phillip didn't break into Bouquets of Love out of frustration and maybe revenge, but the more I think about it, I'm not sure he'd kill over losing the rental property. The most likely suspects are still Thomas Masters and Delila Sommers. I hope that's the direction Detective Acosta is looking in.

Cam and I leave Cup of Jo at four o'clock to go home and get ready for the funeral service. When I saw Mo in the afternoon, she said she and Wes would go with us. She thinks it's a good idea that we go in a group so it doesn't seem like Cam and I are there because we're investigating the case.

I've seen movies and TV shows where the killer shows up at the funeral. If you ask me, it's a dumb move. I'm not sure killers really do return to the scene of the crime as much as they lead you to believe on television. So I'm not sure if I should take a bigger interest in who is at the service or who isn't.

The funeral home parking lot is basically empty. I feel bad that Victoria didn't seem to have many people in her life who cared about her. Of course, Chloe and Hazel are here and the funeral director, but other than them the only other person in attendance is Detective Acosta.

He walks over to us as soon as we arrive. "Interesting seeing you all here."

"I was about to say the same about you," I say.

"It's always good to show up at funerals when a case is ongoing."

"Do you really think the killer would show up to pay his or her respects?" I ask.

"People do crazy things. Some people like the thrill of seeing their handiwork."

He's talking about murder as if it's an accomplishment. But I suppose some killers do see it that way, especially if they get away with it.

"Well, we're here to support Chloe and Hazel. This has been a very rough week for them," I say.

"I heard you arrested Victoria's ex-husband," Mo says.

Detective Acosta nods. "He and his girlfriend are using each other as alibis, though."

I couldn't be more surprised he shared that information with us.

"How do you plan to get around that?" I ask.

"I need evidence. Something to place one or both of them at the scene of the crime."

"Detective, there was a man who was supposed to rent the space before Victoria Masters. He was with Victoria on Sunday. You might want to talk to him to see if he remembers seeing either Thomas Masters or Delila Sommers."

Detective Acosta takes a deep breath, I'm sure to keep his composure since we're at a funeral service. "And how did you happen to discover this?" he asks me.

"Oh, well, I was talking to my landlord today. He mentioned it to me." It's not a total lie since I did talk to Mr. DiAngelo.

"I see. What a coincidence. Do you talk to your landlord often?" he asks.

"He's very nice. I like to check in with him. He was very helpful when Cam and I wanted to renovate Cup of

Jo. And he's looking for a new renter. He asked me to send anyone I came across looking for a rental property his way."

"Maybe I'll give him a call."

"I remember the name he gave me, if you'd like to save yourself some time. It was Phillip Witte. Mr. DiAngelo told me he ultimately decided not to rent to Mr. Witte because he has a record."

Detective Acosta's brow furrows. "A record? For what?"

"Breaking and entering, theft, and possession of stolen goods. I can understand why Mr. DiAngelo decided not to rent to Phillip after he learned about that."

"Yes, I can as well." Detective Acosta laces his hands in front of him. "Tell me, Ms. Coffee, did you happen to speak to Phillip Witte yourself?"

I'll admit he's backed me into a corner with that question. "I did. Back when Mr. DiAngelo expressed his need to rent out the space, I thought I'd try to help and see if the man who inquired about the shop was still interested."

"You didn't know about the criminal charges against him at the time?"

How do I answer that? If I claim I didn't know, not only would I be lying, but Detective Acosta would want to know how I knew the man's name before I spoke with Mr. D. But there's no way he's going to believe Mr. D.

withheld that information when he brought up Phillip either.

"Ms. Coffee?" Detective Acosta says. "Is there a reason you're avoiding my question?"

Yeah, I'm trying to stay out of handcuffs.

CHAPTER FOURTEEN

When I still don't respond, Detective Acosta says, "I think I understand. You're exercising your right not to incriminate yourself, aren't you?"

"Detective," Mo says, and I know from her tone that she's about to get herself into a lot of trouble.

"Maura," Wes says, using her full first name to get her attention.

She stops talking and crosses her arms.

"Nothing to say, Ms. Coffee?" Detective Acosta goads her. "I guess getting tongue tied runs in the family."

Attitude runs in the family. That's for sure, and Mo and I are exercising a lot of restraint right now to not show that.

"Detective, I'd think you'd be happy to receive any information that's helpful to your case," Cam says. "I'm not sure why you treat people who are only doing their civic duty in sharing information that you might deem essential as if they themselves are criminals."

I have to hand it to Cam. He can get his point across while still remaining perfectly calm on the outside and not flat-out calling this guy a jerk. It's a talent I wish I had.

Detective Acosta's face turns pale. I don't think he knows how to react to Cam's comment. "I'm doing my job."

"Glad to hear it because we've had enough experience with law enforcement officers who cared more about their own reputations than protecting this town and its residents. We don't need another detective like that." The previous chief of police resigned because he let his reputation get in the way of a case. And don't get me started on Quentin Perry.

"If you'll excuse me," Detective Acosta says.

"Nicely put," Cam tells me, squeezing my hand.

"I was only following your lead."

"Yeah, way to go, Cam," Mo says. "You kept my sister from totally losing it on him. That's saying something."

Hazel walks past us to the casket. She has a bunch of tissues in her hand, and her face is so red and puffy I swear she must have been crying for hours already. She says goodbye to her sister, and then she gently raises the lid of the casket just enough to slip something inside.

"Did you see that? She put something in the casket with Vicky," I say.

"What was it?" Cam asks.

"I don't know. It looked like a paper of some sort."

"Maybe she wrote her sister a letter," Mo suggests. "You know to help her get over the loss. I know people who have done that."

That does seem like a sweet gesture, not that Vicky would ever get to read the contents of the letter. But I think maybe the action is more for Hazel to find some closure than anything else.

Behind us, the door opens, and a man in his thirties walks in. I don't think I've ever seen him before. He walks right up to the casket.

"Anyone know who that is?" I whisper.

Wes is the first to shake his head. "Never seen him."

"Me either," Mo says.

"Maybe he's from Columbia," Cam suggests.

I'm a little surprised Victoria's former neighbors aren't here. I'm sure they heard about the services. But then again, there's still time for them to show up.

The man spends quite a bit of time at the casket, saying goodbye to Victoria. I'll be honest. I haven't gone near the casket yet. It's closed, thankfully. I don't like looking at dead people. I never wanted that to be the last image I have of someone because I'm afraid it will always be the first image I remember when I think of them, and I prefer to remember people in their prime, not in death. That's just me, though. I get why some people feel the need to see their loved ones one last time.

"Who do you think he is?" Mo asks. "I mean this is a

little weird. He's spending so much time talking to the casket."

I don't want to interrupt him, but I am curious to find out what he's saying. "Stay here," I tell the others.

Cam doesn't let go of my hand when I try to walk away. "You can't eavesdrop on a man who's paying his last respects. It's not right."

"Neither is letting Victoria's death go unsolved." Detective Acosta doesn't have enough evidence. There are so few suspects in this case. It's basically just the ex-husband and his girlfriend. Of course, there's the possibility Victoria's fall was an accident, but either way, I want to feel certain we get to the bottom of this mystery.

Mo jerks a thumb over her shoulder. "Be careful. Detective Likes to Accost You is right over there talking to Chloe Francis."

I smirk. "Detective Likes to Accost You. That's clever, Mo."

She smiles. "My wittiness knows no bounds."

I walk over to the man, remaining a few feet behind him as if I'm in line to pay my respects as well. He's talking so low I can't make out any actual words. His tone is definitely one of grief, though.

I get a tickle in my throat and do my best to cover the need to sneeze, but the man turns around to look at me. "Sorry," I say. "I think I might be allergic to something in here."

"I hope it's not my cologne. I've been told I can go a little heavy when I apply it."

"No worries. Please continue. I didn't mean to interrupt." I gesture toward the casket.

"How did you know Victoria?" the man asks me.

"I own the coffee shop right next to her flower store," I say. I figure it's best to stick to the truth and provide as little information as possible. I don't want to divulge my interest in this case to a perfect stranger. "How about you?"

"I knew her from her previous job."

"Oh?" I don't even know what that was. "You must mean in Columbia."

He nods. "She worked in my bar. She started as my bookkeeper, but she wound up bartending, waiting tables, managing the place, you name it. There was nothing Victoria couldn't do. I don't know what I'm going to do without her."

This strikes me as strange because he lost Victoria as an employee when she moved, not because she died. "I'm very sorry for your loss," I say.

"Thank you. Same to you."

"I'm afraid I hadn't even gotten a chance to get to know her well. I've learned a lot about her from her sisters, though. I've been helping them clear out the flower shop."

"That's nice of you."

"That's how we do things here in Bennett Falls. Everyone helps everyone else out."

"That's a great concept. Maybe I should consider moving here." He looks sad. "Can I ask you a question?"

"Sure."

"Do you know if the police think there was foul play involved in Vicky's death?" His gaze goes to Detective Acosta. "I'm assuming they're considering that possibility if he's here."

"Yes, they are looking into all possibilities."

He inhales deeply and holds the breath for several seconds before releasing it. He knows something.

"I hope you don't mind me saying, but I'm getting the impression that you might have a possibility in mind. Do you know of someone who might have wanted to hurt Victoria?"

"I should have put a stop to it. I told her I would handle it for her, but she insisted she needed to do it herself."

That's strange. Where was that line of thinking when it came to dealing with her abusive husband? Or did his abuse fuel her to take charge of other aspects of her life to compensate for it?

"Mr.—" I pause, realizing I don't know his name.

"Oh, sorry. Evan Gray." He extends his hand, which I shake.

"Joanna Coffee."

"Your name is Coffee and you own a coffee shop?"

"Yes, and yes, it's my real name."

"That's a very fortunate coincidence. It would be ironic if you opened a tea shop instead." He gives a short nervous laugh.

"For the sake of full disclosure, we do serve tea as well," I say.

He smiles at me. "You and Vicky probably would have been great friends."

"I'm sorry we didn't get the chance."

"Mr. Gray, what was it you wanted to put a stop to? Was someone bothering Vicky?" If he says her husband, I'll probably be convinced this case ends with Thomas Masters. It would all add up and make sense.

"His name is Kendrick Frost."

Who?

"He was a regular at my bar. I typically had to cut him off because he never knew his limit. Vicky was good. She'd call him a cab, and when it got to the bar, we'd escort him outside and stick him in the back of the car."

"What did Kendrick do to Vicky that makes you suspect him?" I ask.

I'm suddenly aware of Detective Acosta breathing down my neck. I turn around. "Detective Acosta, this is Evan Gray, Victoria Masters's former employer. He was just telling me about a regular at his bar who gave Vicky a hard time."

"If you're the detective working Vicky's case," Evan says, "I think you should hear this."

"Go on," Detective Acosta says.

"Kendrick Frost was a drunk. He'd come in and hit on Vicky. She told him she was married, but he told her that didn't matter much to him."

"How far did this harassment go?" Detective Acosta asks, his notepad and pen now poised and ready.

"Whenever Vicky would get close enough, Kendrick would grab her arm and not let go. I saw bruises on her arms from it."

It's a toss-up whether Kendrick grabbed her hard enough to bruise her or if the marks were actually from her husband, who, according to Vicky's neighbors, like to hit his wife.

"Did she ever press charges?" Detective Acosta asks.

"Yeah, but his lawyer got them dropped in exchange for Kendrick going to AA and apologizing to Vicky."

I'm surprised the restraining order I found wasn't for Kendrick Frost. It sounds like Vicky needed one for him as well. But then again, maybe part of the deal Kendrick struck with going to AA included not going near Vicky.

"Did he stop harassing her?" I ask, and Detective Acosta gives me some major side eye. Not that I care. I found Evan Gray and got this information out of him. Why shouldn't I get to ask questions?

"He was more discreet about it, but it never really stopped." Evan turns back toward the casket. "I'm telling you this because if Vicky's accident wasn't really an accident, I think it's possible Kendrick followed her here."

"I will personally see that he's found and questioned," Detective Acosta says.

"Thank you. Please find out what happened to Vicky. She deserved so much better than this." His eyes fill with tears.

"You loved her," I say before I can even realize the words escape my lips. I meant to only think them.

Detective Acosta cocks his head. "You were in love with a married woman?"

Evan holds up both hands. "It wasn't like that. Nothing ever happened between us. I knew she was married, and I respected that."

"Was she in love with you?" Detective Acosta asks.

Evan shakes his head. "Our relationship was strictly employer-employee. I never even told her how I felt."

"Are you sure you didn't follow her here and tell her Sunday night?" Detective Acosta asks, putting his notebook and pen away and leveling Evan with a look.

"I was working Sunday night. You can stop by my bar and ask around. Several people saw me and can vouch for me." He pats his pockets. "I'm afraid I don't have a business card on me."

Why would he? It's a funeral.

"What's the name of your bar, and where is it located? I'd like to verify your alibi."

"It's called Gray's, and it's in Columbia, New Jersey."

Detective Acosta nods. "Don't plan any vacations any time soon, Mr. Gray, in case I need to follow up with you."

"I'm not going anywhere. Detective, please promise me you'll follow up with Kendrick Frost. If anyone hurt Vicky, I'd bet money it was Kendrick."

"I assure you I will look into everyone and anyone

connected to Vicky in any way." Detective Acosta turns on his heel and walks away.

"I don't think he likes me very much," Evan says.

"He doesn't like anyone. I'm pretty sure that includes himself, too."

Evan smiles, but it quickly fades. "I should have told her how I felt when I found out she was getting divorced, but I wanted to give her time. I've seen men at the bar who prey on vulnerable women. I didn't want to do that to Vicky. But maybe if I had told her how I feel, she would have stayed in town, and then she'd be alive."

"What if can be a dangerous game to play, Mr. Gray."

"Yes, I suppose you're right. Anyway, I should get going. It was very nice to meet you, Ms. Coffee. If I ever find myself in Bennett Falls again, I'll be sure to stop by your coffee shop."

"It's called Cup of Jo, and it's right on Main Street," I say.

He smirks. "Cup of Jo. I love that."

"Thank you, and I'm very sorry for your loss."

He dips his head and walks out of the funeral home.

"Everything okay?" Cam asks, coming over to me. "It took all my might not to join you when Detective Acosta butted in."

"You mean it took all my might," Mo says. "I had to hold him back."

I fill them in on everything Evan Gray told me.

"It sounds like you have a new suspect to look into,"

Mo says. "I'll get you an address for Kendrick Frost tonight."

"Thanks, Mo. I want to beat Detective Acosta to Frost in the morning."

"You don't think he'll go question him this evening?" Wes asks.

"He's out of jurisdiction, and Detective Acosta isn't going to risk doing anything that might get him in hot water. He'll have to run this by Chief Harvey, who will have to contact his buddy at the Columbia Police Department before Detective Acosta even steps foot out of the state."

I just hope me poking around and asking Frost questions doesn't send him running before Detective Acosta can arrest him for murder.

CHAPTER FIFTEEN

The one good thing about drunks is you're pretty certain to find them home asleep early in the morning since they were most likely out late drinking at the bar the night before. Last night, Jamar told me he'd make sure things were okay at Cup of Jo. Cam got up at three in the morning to go to work and get all the baking done before opening. I met Jamar, Robin, and Tyler at six to get them situated. Then Cam and I headed out at six thirty to be at Kendrick's place a little after seven.

Mo had no trouble getting his address, and she learned that Kendrick Frost is an actor. I'm guessing not a very good one since he lives in a small town instead of in New York City or Los Angeles. But maybe he tried that life and failed, and that's why he's drowning his sorrows in alcohol every night.

We drive past Gray's bar on the way to Kendrick's house. It's a cute little place. There's an outdoor Tiki bar and a small patio area. The building itself is also small, but it's definitely not a hole in the wall by any means.

Kendrick lives about three miles from the bar. Quite convenient for him. His home looks like it was meant to be a summer cottage that was converted to a year-round property. The lawn is actually well maintained, and there's even a garden out front.

Cam pulls up the gravel driveway and parks. "I wasn't expecting this," he says as we walk up to the front door.

"Me either. I thought we'd be encountering a disheveled house and overgrown lawn."

"Maybe he hires a landscaper."

Doubtful. Out of work actors can't exactly afford landscapers.

Cam knocks on the front door. I'm fully prepared to have to knock several times to wake up the drunken man inside, but the door opens only seconds later.

The man standing in front of us is wearing an ironed button-down shirt and khaki pants that look recently pressed. "Can I help you?"

"We're looking for Kendrick Frost," I say, assuming Mo somehow gave us the wrong address.

"That's me."

I probably closely resemble a cartoon character whose jaw falls down to the ground.

He laughs. "Clearly I'm not what you were expecting."

"Sorry, but no. We heard about you from some people at Gray's Bar," Cam says.

"Oh. Well, that certainly explains it."

AA must be working wonders for him.

"I'm turning over a new leaf. Gave up drinking and the bar scene."

"Because of Vicky?" I ask.

"What about her?" He narrows his eyes at me. "I haven't gone near her in weeks, so if she told you something, she's lying."

"She's dead," I say. "She died a week ago."

He runs a hand through his hair. "I had no idea."

"When was the last time you saw her?" I ask.

"Right before she quit working at the bar, I guess. That was about two weeks ago."

I never asked Evan Gray when he last saw Kendrick. "Did you stop going to the bar around that time?" I ask. That would prove he was only there to harass Vicky.

"Yeah, I had a little problem with alcohol. I'm in AA now, getting sober. Bars aren't really great places to hang out when you're trying to stay away from booze, you know?"

"Of course," Cam says. "It's great that AA is working out for you."

"We heard you sometimes gave Vicky a hard time when you'd had too much to drink." I'm trying to keep Evan Gray's name out of this. I don't want Kendrick to retaliate for Evan giving us information about his drunken behavior.

Kendrick puts his hands in his pockets and looks down at his shoes. "I'm not proud of my actions. Vicky didn't deserve what I did to her."

"What did you do to her?" Is he confessing to killing her? Maybe that's what scared him straight. It's possible he showed up in Bennett Falls, completely drunk, and he fought with Vicky. He might have lashed out in rage and accidentally killed her. Her death could very well have been manslaughter. An act of passion in a heated moment that led to Vicky's death.

"I grabbed her a few times. I know now that I shouldn't have touched her. I feel awful about it." He shakes his head. "I was a different person when I was drinking. I'm getting help, though. Nothing like that will ever happen again."

A patrol car pulls into the driveway. I turn to see Detective Acosta behind the wheel. He got here much sooner than I ever anticipated, which means he spent last night going through all the proper channels to get himself here without stepping on any toes with the Columbia Police Department.

"What's going on?" Kendrick asks us as if we planned this.

I look at Cam, wondering how we're going to explain this. Detective Acosta isn't just going to look the other way this time. We are clearly interfering with his investigation.

Detective Acosta gets out of the patrol car and storms over to us. "Ms. Coffee, Mr. Turner, leave. Now."

"What's going on? Who are you?" Kendrick asks.

"Are you Kendrick Frost?" Detective Acosta asks.

"Yes. And again, I'm going to ask who you are."

"Detective Acosta with the Bennett Falls Police Department. I need to speak to you about the death of Victoria Masters."

Kendrick points to Cam and me. "I just told them I didn't even know Vicky was dead."

"Well, they aren't police officers, so you're going to have to tell me." He turns to Cam and me. "You two can leave right this second, or you can take a seat in the back of my patrol car and wait for me to bring you back to the station and arrest you for interfering with my case. Your choice."

"Hang on," Kendrick says. "What is going on? What investigation?"

"He thinks you might have murdered Victoria Masters," I say.

Kendrick holds up both hands. "No way. I haven't seen her in weeks. She quit bartending, and my job was done."

"Your job?" I ask.

Kendrick sighs, and that's when everything clicks into place for me.

"You're an actor. You're not a drunk at all, are you? You were acting. But why?"

Cam gives me a quizzical look, not having reached the same conclusion about Kendrick.

Kendrick holds up both hands. "Okay. I'll tell you the

truth." He pauses and takes a deep breath before continuing. "This guy paid me to harass his wife."

"You were paid?" Detective Acosta asks.

"That's right."

"The man who paid you was Thomas Masters," I say.

Kendrick nods. "He didn't give me his name at first, but I figured it out. When Vicky called the cops on me, I needed a lawyer. It was Masters's colleague who represented me. He made a deal where I had to promise to stay away from Vicky and go to AA. I had no problem with that because I wasn't a drunk anyway. I don't even like beer. And going to AA has helped me research for a role I'm planning to audition for, so it worked out for everyone. I even got enough money to fix up this place."

"What exactly did Thomas Masters hire you to do?" Detective Acosta asks.

"He said I needed to make inappropriate comments about Vicky when other people were around to hear it. And he said I should grab her arm sometimes too and not let go until she threatened to call the police on me." He shakes his head. "I think I grabbed her too hard once though, because I saw marks on her afterward. I felt awful."

Thomas Masters was trying to cover up the fact that he beat his wife by hiring an actor to pretend to be some crazy man that abused her at the bar. He set up Kendrick Frost to take the fall for the marks on Victoria's arms.

"Mr. Frost, I'm going to need you to come to the

station and make a statement," Detective Acosta says. "The Columbia PD are aware of the case and are allowing me to use their station while I'm here. We can go there now."

"I'm not in trouble, am I? I mean, I'm following the judge's orders from my harassment case with Vicky. You aren't going to arrest me, are you?"

"No. I need to have you put on record what you just told me about Thomas Masters."

"You think he killed her?"

"And possibly tried to frame you," Detective Acosta says.

That's what Kendrick needed to hear to fully cooperate. "Yeah, I'll tell you everything you want to know. I'm not going to jail for what this guy did."

Detective Acosta turns to Cam and me. "I mean it. Get out of here. You're lucky I just caught the break I need in this case, or I would be bringing you two back to the BFPD right now."

"We're going," Cam says.

We don't waste any time getting back in the SUV and on the road.

"We got lucky," Cam says.

"I know. And it looks like this case is wrapped up. Thomas Masters might have even planned the entire thing out. I mean he hired Kendrick Frost to publicly abuse Victoria. It not only covered up the signs of his own abuse, but it set up a suspect in case Victoria's death wasn't ruled an accident."

"Kendrick said Masters works at a law firm. He knows enough about the law to cover his tracks."

Yeah, and it also explains why he was so insistent on keeping up appearances. News that he beat his wife would ruin his reputation as a lawyer. "With Delila Sommers living in the town where Victoria moved, it was easy enough for Thomas to keep tabs on Victoria and know when to strike."

"It seems almost cliché, you know? The ex being the guilty party."

I agree, but what really bugs me is that Detective Acosta was right all along about Thomas Masters. This is going to make him arrogant, but then again, maybe it will get him to stop acting like he has something to prove. He did let Cam and me go after all.

By evening, Thomas Masters's arrest for Vicky's murder is all over the news. Cup of Jo is buzzing with people, and they all want to hear every detail of the case from Cam and me.

"Come on, Jo," Mickey whines. "You know I have to get to work soon. My shift at the high school starts in half an hour. Throw me a bone."

"Sorry, Mickey, but credit goes to Detective Acosta. He should be the one to tell the story. Feel free to ask him yourself, and then you can tell everyone else." I'm going to let Detective Acosta take full credit since he did suspect Thomas Masters from the start and because I don't want to get even more on his bad side by allowing people to think I helped solve the case. Even if I did.

"I thought we were tight, Jo," Mickey says.

"We are, Mickey, but I can't help you this time. Cam and I weren't there when Detective Acosta brought Kendrick Frost in for his full statement."

Mickey huffs but walks back to his table.

As if he sensed everyone here was talking about him, Detective Acosta walks into Cup of Jo. Mickey jumps up from his seat. "Detective, let me be the first to congratulate you on solving your first case here in Bennett Falls." He extends his hand.

Detective Acosta looks very uncomfortable as he shakes Mickey's hand. "Thank you, but I was only doing my job."

"Modest, too," Mickey says, looking around to get everyone's attention. "It's a big improvement from his predecessor."

"Excuse me," Detective Acosta says, walking past Mickey and up to the counter. "You're open later than usual today."

"Keeping tabs on me?" I ask.

"Merely making an observation."

"What can I get for you?"

He looks up at the chalkboard menu on the wall. "What do you recommend?"

"How about a mocha to celebrate closing the case?"

"Sounds good." He clears his throat as I turn around to make his drink.

"Something on your mind, Detective?"

"Actually, yes. I did my research before coming here. I

know about your history with Detective Perry and your involvement in several cases with the BFPD. What I don't know is why you do it."

"Do what?" I ask, adding the whipped cream to his drink and sprinkling it with cocoa powder. I turn around and hand it to him.

"Get involved. What's in it for you?"

I lean down on the counter in front of me. "This town has been my home for my entire life. I don't want to see anything bad happen to it or anyone who lives here. So I guess when something bad does happen, I feel the need to fix it."

"Hmm. And here I thought dating an officer of the law gave you the detective bug."

"That, too. I guess it was one of the few things Quentin and I had in common."

"I take it things didn't end well with you two." He sips his mocha.

"I'd rather not discuss my previous relationship. I'm quite happy with my life now."

"You and Mr. Turner do seem to be two peas in a pod."

I'm pretty sure he actually means two thorns in his side, but he's trying to be civil. "Detective, I know Chief Harvey doesn't allow consultants, but working here has certain advantages. People talk. I hear a lot of things, and I don't think I'd be a good citizen if I let those things slide without doing anything."

"This is why you asked about C.I.s," he says.

"I'm not looking to be your confidential informant. Honestly, none of my customers would think there was anything confidential about it. But if you promise not to point your finger in my direction, I'll pass along any information I find out that might be helpful to you."

"Are you proposing a truce?" he asks.

"Does that sound so awful?"

He smirks. "No, I suppose not. But I won't turn my head the other way if you break the law, Ms. Coffee."

"It's Jo."

He inhales deeply. "Jo."

"I'm not asking you to let me get away with breaking the law. I'm asking you to allow me to help if I can."

"Fair enough, but maybe we keep this arrangement between us." He means he doesn't want word of this getting back to Chief Harvey. Neither do I.

I nod.

He places a ten-dollar bill on the counter. "Keep the change." He turns and walks out.

"Did I hear that right?" Cam asks, walking out of the kitchen.

"How did I know you were eavesdropping?" I ask him, placing the money in the register and the change in the tip jar.

Cam wraps an arm around me. "Well, let's see. The new detective in town hasn't been the nicest to you, so there was the possibility he was going to cause trouble. I had to be prepared to step in and save you."

"Save me, huh?"

"Okay, poor choice of words. You never need saving."

That's not exactly true. I've found myself needing saving several times in the past, mostly thanks to murder investigations.

"But then I realized the gorgeous new detective was being nice to you, and that might have concerned me even more," he admits, looking down at his feet.

I tip his chin up so he's looking at me. "As far as I'm concerned, I married the most gorgeous man alive, so I don't care what the new detective happens to look like."

He gives me a kiss. "Good answer."

Movement through the front window draws my attention. Hazel is carrying a box into Bouquets of Love. "Oh, I didn't realize Hazel was still in town. I want to go say goodbye to her before she leaves."

"Tell her goodbye for me, too," he says. "I have to go finish cleaning up for the night."

"Okay. I'll be right back." I walk next door and knock. I don't see Hazel inside, though, so I try the door, which is unlocked.

"Hazel?" I call. "It's Jo Coffee." I walk toward the back of the store. Did she go upstairs? "Hazel?" I call again.

A piercing scream comes from upstairs. "Hazel!"

CHAPTER SIXTEEN

I run up the stairs to find Hazel in the storage room. "Are you okay?" I ask, looking around at the empty space.

She turns toward me. "There's a rat." She points toward the corner where a rat is crouched.

"Oh." I will my heart to stop racing now that I know she's okay. "You scared me." Part of me thought we were wrong about Thomas Masters, and Hazel stumbled upon the real killer. "I can call someone to remove it for you."

"I'm leaving anyway. It's fine."

"What are you doing here?" I ask. "I thought everything was taken care of with the flower shop, and you'd be on your way back home."

She starts to cry again. "I should be heading back home by now. I was supposed to right after the service. I just can't bring myself to do it."

I think I understand what she's going through. Leaving means accepting Vicky is gone. She's not ready to do that. "Maybe you should stay with Chloe for a while," I suggest.

She wipes her nose with the back of her hand. "I think she's getting sick of me. Chloe wants to get back to life as usual. She keeps saying that's what Vicky would want us to do, but how can I?"

I wrap one arm around her shoulders. "Everyone grieves in different ways. Chloe might need to keep busy so she doesn't spend all her time crying. It's probably how she's dealing with her pain."

"I want Vicky to know how sorry I am."

"Sorry for what?" I ask.

"The last time I spoke to Vicky, we argued." Hazel sniffles. "I feel awful about it, but I was so angry." Her face turns red as she recalls the memory.

"What happened, Hazel? What did you and Vicky fight about?"

"It was over him. Thomas. She dropped the restraining order against him. Can you believe that?"

"Maybe she was scared he'd retaliate in some way. Fear can motivate people to do a lot of things."

"It would have kept him away from us."

Us? Hazel doesn't even live in Bennett Falls. She's only here temporarily. So what does she mean by that? "I'm not sure I'm following."

"He always finds her no matter where she goes."

"Like when she moved here," I say. "Was there another time it happened?"

"Yeah. She moved to Arameda first. He found her

there. Then she came here, thinking with Chloe in town at least she wouldn't be alone if Thomas came looking for her again."

That makes sense. But if she was this scared of Thomas, why didn't she file the restraining order? I have to agree with Hazel there.

She walks around the storage space. "Do you know why she was clearing this space out up here?"

I shake my head.

"Vicky always took care of me. Our parents were in their forties when they had me. I was the surprise baby." She rolls her eyes. "In other words, I wasn't exactly wanted. It's not like my parents decided to raise another child at that age. It just happened."

"Chloe was ten by then, right?" I ask.

Hazel scoffs. "Chloe's been saying she's thirty-five for the past five years."

She lied about her age? I guess it's not all that uncommon for women to do that as they get older. "Are you saying she's actually fifteen years older than you are?"

Hazel nods. "Vicky was ten years younger than her. Another 'oops' on my parents' part. I think we bonded more because of that. Chloe was the only child they actually planned for, and she was practically out of the house by the time I was born. I don't really remember her at all. She went to college at eighteen and never looked back."

"What about Chloe and Vicky? Were they close?"

Chloe let Vicky move in with her here in Bennett Falls, and from what Hazel just told me, the reason why Chloe suggested Bennett Falls to Vicky in the first place was so they could be close.

"Not growing up, but once Vicky was an adult and out of our parents' house, she and Chloe connected more." A tear falls from her eye. "And then our parents were killed in a boating accident in Florida. I swear they moved the second I turned eighteen. It was like they considered their duty of raising me done as soon as I was legally an adult. They packed up and moved two days after I graduated high school."

Ouch. That sounds rough. But at least Hazel had Vicky. That must be why her death has been so hard on her. "I'm so sorry, Hazel."

"Vicky was going to let me live here above the store. I wanted to be close to her again. Thomas took her away from me for too long."

And now he took Vicky away for good. My heart is breaking for Hazel. "Is there anything I can do?"

She shakes her head. "I just want to tell Vicky how much I love her and how sorry I am."

"That's why you wrote her the letter, right?"

"What letter?" she asks.

"The one you put in her casket," I say.

"You saw that?" She looks embarrassed by it.

"I thought it was a great idea. Hopefully it gives you some closure."

She lets out a deep breath. "I should go. I was just

returning a box of things that belonged to the former renter. I guess she accidentally left them behind."

"Oh, I'll let Mr. DiAngelo know. He can contact Samantha." I could too, but I'm sure she'd invite me to come visit and bring the box with me. I'm not ready for that.

"Thanks. You've been really great, Jo. I wish…" Sobs cut off her words. "I should go." She hurries down the stairs.

Cam is waiting for me when I walk outside. "All locked up," he says, gesturing to Cup of Jo. "Hazel seemed like she was in a hurry."

"I think it really upsets her to be anywhere near the place where Vicky died. I feel awful for her. She feels like she has no one left since she and Chloe aren't close."

"Poor girl."

We drive home, stopping for takeout on the way because I'm too tired to cook. It's been a very long day.

I'm dragging Monday morning. I should have had a great night sleep since the case is closed, but something is bothering me. I have this weird feeling.

Detective Acosta comes in for coffee and asks me if I have a minute to talk. The look Cam gives him through the kitchen window is nothing short of jealousy. I hate that Cam thinks he has any reason to be jealous. I'm the most loyal person there is. I don't really think it has to do with trusting me, though. I think he doesn't trust Detective Acosta.

"Delila Sommers came to the station this morning asking to take a lie detector test to prove she was with Thomas the night Victoria Masters was killed," Detective Acosta says.

"Did you let her take the test?" I ask.

He nods. "She passed with flying colors."

"Are you doubting your case against Thomas now?"

He huffs. "It would be one thing if I found the restraining order in his possession. It could prove he broke in and stole it and that he had motive for killing Vicky."

"But he didn't have it. Where is it then?" I ask.

"I wish I knew. He's swearing he never took it."

"Sounds like you need to find it if you want to prove his guilt."

"If you hear anything…" He doesn't finish the statement, but I nod anyway. "Thanks." He gets up and leaves.

"What was that about?" Cam asks, walking over to the table.

"The missing restraining order and Thomas Masters's airtight alibi."

"Are you saying the case isn't closed after all?"

"No, I don't think it is."

I spend the rest of my morning trying to go over every aspect of the case again while also serving my customers. Tyler can tell I'm distracted, so he's doing his best to help as many people as possible before I can screw up their orders. I'm completely zoned and staring out the window when a woman carrying a box walks by Cup of Jo. She reminds me of Hazel returning Sam's things the night before.

I get an idea and rush into the kitchen to find Cam. To my surprise, Mo and Wes are in the kitchen with him, trying a new recipe.

"This is heavenly, Cam," Mo says.

"Thanks. I used the same mousse from my Cups of Heaven in the center."

"Jo, come try this," Mo says.

"Remember how I saw Hazel put something in Victoria's casket?" I ask them all, ignoring Mo, who is holding out some puff pastry to me.

Cam nods. "Yeah, why?"

"What if it wasn't a letter to Vicky? What if it was the restraining order?"

"Why would Hazel have the restraining order?" Mo asks.

"I don't know, but if Thomas Masters and Delila Sommers don't have it, Hazel might."

"You said she's afraid of Thomas Masters," Cam says. "Maybe she thought she could get him to agree to stay far away from her if she turned over the restraining order to him so no one would find out he abused Vicky."

"You mean like an agreement to stay away in exchange for her silence," Wes says.

"Yes," I say. "Hazel was scared, and she kept saying

she wanted Vicky to know she was sorry. I think they fought about the restraining order right before Vicky died."

"Why would it even matter now that Victoria is dead, though?" Mo asks.

"I don't know, but I suppose news of the restraining order could have tainted Thomas's reputation. It would have led some people to think he killed Victoria to prevent her from filing the restraining order with a judge."

"You mean before he was arrested for exactly that," Cam says.

I nod.

"But if that's why Hazel took the restraining order, why didn't she give it to Thomas?" Wes asks.

"Maybe she had second thoughts." Mo shrugs.

I shake my head. "No. She told me she hated the fact that Vicky never stood up for herself. Hazel wouldn't do the same thing. She wouldn't cower down to Thomas. And if she wanted to turn the restraining order over to him, why would she stage a break-in?"

"You think she was trying to make it look like Thomas broke in?" Cam asks.

"It makes sense, right? She could have grabbed the paperwork from the filing cabinet and given it to him without anyone knowing. But staging a break-in had to be meant to implicate him. She wanted him to be arrested."

"And she knew Detective Acosta was lacking evidence against Thomas," Cam says.

"Okay, I guess that all makes sense," Mo says, "but why would Hazel put the restraining order in the casket to be buried with her sister instead of planting it in Thomas's possession to make him look guilty?"

"Oh my goodness!"

"What?" Mo asks.

There is another reason. One that explains why Hazel has been taking Vicky's death so hard and why she's having a hard time leaving Bennett Falls. "What if Thomas didn't kill Vicky?"

"What do you mean? Of course, he did," Mo says.

"There's no proof. Yes, he was an abusive husband, and he paid Kendrick Frost to harass Vicky so he could get away with that abuse, but I'm not sure he actually killed Vicky. Too much points to this being an accident or as close to one as possible."

"Close how?" Wes asks. "You mean like manslaughter?"

"That's exactly what I mean. Hazel told me she fought with Vicky over the restraining order. What if that fight got physical, and Hazel pushed Vicky? Shoved her so hard that Vicky fell down the stairs and broke her neck?"

Cam rubs his chin. "That does makes sense. It explains Hazel's behavior. And maybe giving Vicky the restraining order in the end was her way of apologizing since it's what started the fight that led to Vicky's death."

"But she staged the break-in," Mo says.

"Yes, because I think she wanted Thomas to pay for hurting her sister. She planned to set him up so he'd go to jail for murder. But her conscience got the best of her, and she never planted the restraining order on him."

"Wow," Wes says. "If this is true…"

"I have to tell Detective Acosta." I'm pretty sure Hazel is hoping I figure it out. "She'd been trying to confess to me yesterday, and I totally missed it." She wants me to do what she can't bring herself to. Turn her in.

CHAPTER SEVENTEEN

Detective Acosta leans back in his desk chair. "You have no proof of any of this."

"We might. If the restraining order is inside Victoria Masters's casket, it proves Hazel was the one who stole it and staged the break-in." I'm also convinced she's going to confess if we get our hands on that paperwork.

"You want me to dig up a body that was put in the ground last night?" he asks me, twirling a pen between his fingers.

I lean across the desk and whisper. "I did my research. We know why you left L.A. Do you really want to chance that you have the wrong man here?"

Cam nods. "She's right. This could destroy you."

Detective Acosta sighs and stands up. "Give me a minute. I need to speak to Chief Harvey."

"We should go. I don't want to get you in trouble for talking to us."

"It's fine. You had information. Bringing it to my attention was the right thing to do. But you're free to go now. I'll handle it from here."

I nod. I can only imagine how Chloe will react when Detective Acosta shows up with a warrant to remove her sister's body from the ground. I don't think I can stomach the torture she'll be put through during that, and then finding out her other sister was the cause of Vicky's death...

Cam and I go back to Cup of Jo.

"I might like this arrangement," Cam says. "Us giving information to Detective Acosta and letting him handle the hard stuff. This is how it should be." He kisses the side of my head. "I have baking to do."

"I've decided to call Samantha about the box of stuff after all. I should be the one to do it. I'll just offer to ship it to her."

Cam smiles at me. "You're a good person, Joanna Coffee. The absolute best."

I return the smile before walking next door. I don't stop to consider the place will be locked up until I'm in front of the door. I stop and sigh. At least I tried to be the bigger person. For some reason, I try the doorknob before leaving. It turns easily in my hand. I guess I forgot to lock the door behind me last night after Hazel ran out. I should definitely go in and make sure nothing was vandalized since it would be my fault for leaving the store unlocked.

I open the door and step inside. Since the place is

mostly empty, there's really nothing for anyone to steal. And there doesn't look like there's any damage either. I walk to the back to make sure everything looks okay there, too.

Sobbing from upstairs draws my attention. "Chloe?" I call, thinking she must have come by and I'm not responsible for the unlocked door. I start up the steps.

The door to the upstairs room is slightly ajar, and I push it fully open. But it's not Chloe inside. It's Hazel.

"Hazel, what are you doing here?"

"I tried, Jo. I really did. But I can't do it. It's my fault. It's all my fault, and I can't leave."

"It's okay." I don't think she meant to hurt her sister. "I understand."

"No, you don't. It wasn't Thomas. He didn't push her. I did. Me." She's sobbing, and her arms flail at her sides. "I was so angry. She refused to stand up for herself. He was ruining her life and mine, but she wouldn't file that stupid restraining order. I found it that night. In the filing cabinet. When I confronted her, she told me I didn't understand. That I'm a naïve kid who thinks the police can solve all our problems."

"She was scared. She didn't want Thomas to know where she was. I think she believed holding on to the restraining order was enough to keep him away if he did find her."

"But he already had! His girlfriend lives here. He showed up on Sunday. He was here. He left when I came."

"You didn't tell the police you saw him here. Why?" That would have implicated him.

"If I did, he would have told them I was here, too. I kept my mouth shut because I knew he'd never admit to being here unless he had to."

Her silence ensured his.

"I didn't mean to hurt her. She got me so angry, and I just reacted. She came up here to my room. The room she promised me. She told me if I didn't like the way she was handling things, I shouldn't move in here. But I'd already given up my apartment back home. I had nowhere else to go, and she knew it."

"She stood up to you," I say.

Hazel swipes at her wet cheeks. "Yeah. She refused to stand up to him, but she had no problem doing it with me. Her sister. I was trying to help her, and she lashed out at me."

"And you got angry."

"I followed her up here and grabbed her. I wanted her to look at me. To look me in the eyes and listen to what I had to say." She pauses for a moment, trying to compose herself, but tears stream down her cheeks.

I remain silent, letting her tell her story in her own time.

"I grabbed her hair and yanked her back." A sharp inhale cuts her off for a moment. "She fell backward. I tried to reach for her, but her momentum... I couldn't stop her. She hit her head on the stair and tumbled down to the bottom. From the way her neck was bent, I knew it was broken." She's shaking uncontrollably now. "She was just staring up at me. Every time I think about her, that's what I see. Her lifeless eyes staring at me, accusing me. But I didn't mean for it to happen."

"I know you didn't. It's okay, Hazel. You can go with me to see Detective Acosta. We'll tell him what happened."

"I just want her to forgive me."

"She will. All you have to do is tell the truth."

She inhales a shaky breath. "You'll go with me?"

I nod and reach for her. She lets me wrap an arm around her shoulders.

"I'm so sorry," she says.

"So she just confessed?" Mo asks at dinner.

"Yeah, I think she's been wanting to get that off her chest for a while. She was too scared to go through with it on her own, though."

"Will it be ruled an accident?" Wes asks.

"Since the act of violence happened in the heat of the moment, Detective Acosta said she'll be tried for manslaughter, but it all depends on how the jury sees it."

"This case has been crazy," Cam says.

"You can say that again."

"At least you seem to be on good terms with Detective Acosta now. I might have to think of a new nickname for him." She pouts. "I really liked Detective Likes to Accost You, too. It was a solid name."

Wes pats her shoulder. "You'll come up with another one that's equally as good."

"Did they actually exhume Victoria's body?" Cam asks.

"Yeah, they had to recover the restraining order because it's evidence. Hazel confessed to everything, though."

"What about Thomas Masters?" Wes asks.

"Detective Acosta took Hazel's statement, and he's being charged with assault and harassment."

"I'm glad he's not getting off scot-free," Mo says.

"Don't forget Kendrick Frost already confessed to his part in Thomas's plan to hurt Victoria," Cam says. "Masters will have to answer for that as well."

"Then I guess justice has been served yet again thanks to all of us." Mo raises her cup of coffee in the air.

It's sort of become our job to restore order to this town. "How about we toast to an uneventful evening?" I suggest. "I could really use one of those."

"Hear, hear," Cam says. "I'm thinking we never should have come back from our honeymoon.

"Take a second one," Mo suggests.

"I think we've left Jamar, Robin, and Tyler to take care of Cup of Jo enough lately. Besides, I love my job, and it doesn't matter where Cam and I are, as long as we're together."

"Gag," Mo says. "Wes, that's our cue to leave. They're being all lovey-dovey, and I really don't want to lose my dinner."

"See you tomorrow," I say as they get up from the couch.

"Goodnight," Wes says.

"I guess it's time for bed," Cam says. "Unless you want me to stay up with you for a bit."

"I'll settle for lying in your arms while you fall asleep."

"Deal," he says, helping me off the couch. "And in case I haven't mentioned it lately, I really love being married to you."

I loop my arms around his neck and give him a kiss. "It's my favorite part of my life."

"Really? Even better than knowing you solved a woman's death?"

"I'll admit I like helping the people in this town, but you're still my favorite person in the world, Camden Turner. And you're all mine." Unlike the other uncertainties in my life, my feelings for Cam will never be a mystery to me.

If you enjoyed the book, please consider leaving a review. And look for *Bicerin and Bloodshed*, coming soon!

You can stay up-to-date on all of Kelly's releases by subscribing to her newsletter: http://bit.ly/2pvYT07

CUP OF JO SERIES

PIPER ASHWELL PSYCHIC P.I. SERIES

Murder is in the Eye of the Beholder
Between A Vision and a Hard Case
There's More Than One Way to Sense a Killer
A Mental Picture Paints A Thousand Crimes

SHORTER SERIES

Holidays Can Be Murder Series
Valentine Victim
Fourth of July Fatality
Halloween Homicide
Traumatic Temp Agency Series
Corpse at the Candy Shop
Tragedy at the Toy Shop
Bludgeoning at the Boutique

Madison Kramer Mysteries
Manuscripts and Murder
Sequels and Serial Killers
Fiction and Felonies

WRITING AS USA TODAY
BESTSELLING ROMANCE AUTHOR
ASHELYN DRAKE

The Time for Us
Second Chance Summer
It Was Always You (Love Chronicles #1)
I Belong With You (Love Chronicles #2)
Since I Found You (Love Chronicles #3)
Reignited
After Loving You (New Adult romance)
Campus Crush (New Adult romance)
Falling For You (Free prequel to *Perfect For You*)
Perfect For You (Young Adult contemporary romance)
Our Little Secret (Young Adult contemporary romance)

ACKNOWLEDGMENTS

As always, many thanks to my editor, Patricia Bradley, for all your feedback and suggestions on this series. To my cover designer, Ali Winters at Red Umbrella Graphic Designs, you blew me away with this cover. I couldn't love it more. Thank you.

To my family and friends, thank you for your continued support. To my VIP reader group and my ARC team, I'm so grateful for you guys. Thank you for reading my work and helping me spread the word about my books. And thank you to YOU, my reader. I wouldn't have a career without you.

ABOUT THE AUTHOR

Kelly Hashway fully admits to being one of the most accident-prone people on the planet, but luckily, she gets to write about female sleuths who are much more coordinated than she is. Maybe it was growing up watching *Murder, She Wrote* that instilled a love of mystery, but she spends her days writing cozy mysteries. Kelly's also a sucker for first love, which is why she writes romance under the pen name Ashelyn Drake. When she's not writing, Kelly works as an editor and also as Mom, which she believes is a job title that deserves to be capitalized.